Hearts **racing.**

Blood **pumping.**

Pulses **accelerating.**

Falling in love can be a blur... especially at 180 mph!

So if you crave the thrill of the chase—on and off the track—you'll love

SPEED BUMPS

by Ken Casper!

When Vaughn looked up and saw Gabby walking toward them, he felt a strange lightness in his chest, a euphoria he realized a moment later was completely inappropriate.

She was one of his drivers, and he was reacting to her as a woman. The logical side of his brain tried mightily to categorize her as a key member of his team, but his psyche knew better.

Gabby O'Farrell was a woman he'd had dinner with, gotten to talk to about something other than cars and driving. He almost wished now he hadn't. Almost.

He respected her driving skills, and he admired her gumption in taking on a challenge that few people, male or female, dared accept. Until last Friday evening, he'd been able to treat her as a business associate, and he had to continue to treat her that way.

He didn't want to think of her as a woman right now.

Dear Reader,

Some things are uniquely American, made in the U.S.A. Football, basketball and of course NASCAR. If you've ever been to a NASCAR race, you know nothing quite compares with the thrill of the ground vibrating under you, the smell of hot asphalt and burning rubber, the sight and sound of cars covered with colorful decals screaming around a high-banked track. And if you haven't been to a NASCAR race, you've missed something really special.

If you are a fan, chances are your family is, too, 'cause NASCAR is a family sport. Maybe you all have different favorites among drivers, crew chiefs and teams, but when the checkered flag flutters, everybody cheers for the winner. That's the way NASCAR is. Each of us may have our preferences, but the bottom line is that they're all good guys out there.

When I was invited to contribute to this NASCAR series, I felt honored and privileged. NASCAR is a very special family, and the challenge of setting a tale in such an exciting world was one I couldn't pass up. I love playing the what-if game. I'm a fiction writer, after all. So what if a woman made it to the NASCAR NEXTEL Cup Series? Not completely far-fetched. And what if she then fell in love with her boss? Well, things like that have been known to happen. Put them together and, well, you have a story that's got its own dynamics.

I hope you enjoy this book and the series. Talk about things uniquely American—romance set amidst the excitement of NASCAR! It doesn't get any better.

I'm always glad to hear from readers, and I'll be particularly anxious to get your reaction to this story and the NASCAR series in general. You can write me at P.O. Box 61511, San Angelo, TX 76904-9998. See you at the races.

Ken Casper

NASCAR®

SPEED BUMPS

Ken Casper

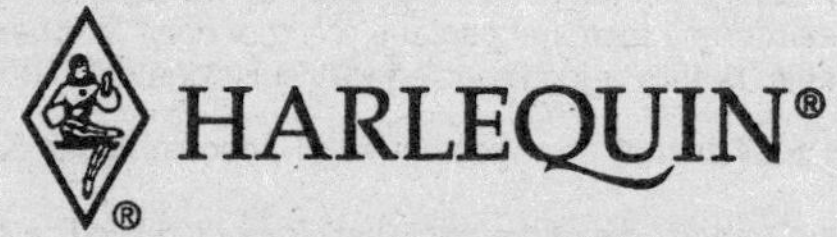

TORONTO • NEW YORK • LONDON
AMSTERDAM • PARIS • SYDNEY • HAMBURG
STOCKHOLM • ATHENS • TOKYO • MILAN • MADRID
PRAGUE • WARSAW • BUDAPEST • AUCKLAND

ISBN-13: 978-0-373-21774-8
ISBN-10: 0-373-21774-9

SPEED BUMPS

Kenneth Casper is acknowledged as the author of this work.

This edition published by arrangement with Harlequin Books S.A.

www.eHarlequin.com

Printed in U.S.A.

KEN CASPER,

aka K.N. Casper, figures his writing career started back in the sixth grade when a teacher ordered him to write a "theme" explaining his misbehavior over the previous semester. To his teacher's chagrin, he enjoyed stringing just the right words together to justify his less than stellar performance. That's not to say he's been telling tall tales to get out of scrapes ever since, but...

Born and raised in New York City, Ken is now a transplanted Texan. He and Mary, his wife of over thirty years, own a horse farm in San Angelo. Along with their two dogs, six cats and eight horses—at last count!—they board and breed horses and Mary teaches English riding. She's a therapeutic riding instructor for the handicapped, as well.

Life is never dull. Their two granddaughters visit several times a year and feel right at home with the Casper menagerie. Grandpa and Mimi do everything they can to make sure their visits will be lifelong fond memories. After all, isn't that what grandparents are for?

You can keep up with Ken and his books on his Web site at www.kncasper.com.

To Greg and Lori Kerr,
fans and inspirers who got there first

To Marsha Zinberg, thanks for the opportunities

CHAPTER ONE

ENERGY PULSED AROUND HER. Through her. Inside her. If she didn't need both hands on the steering wheel, she would have raised her fist and shouted, "Yes!"

Last weekend she'd driven Vaughn Steiner's Number 111 car in Daytona. The Super Bowl of stock car racing. She'd come in a respectable, if not terribly impressive, twenty-second out of forty-three.

Now here she was at the race track in California and doing considerably better. From her twelfth-position start in the pack of forty-three, she'd moved up to third place. Third place!

That could change in a heartbeat, of course. A blown tire. Worse, a blown engine. Or the inevitable crash.

"Pit stop, Gabby," the voice in her helmet announced. Mack Roberts, her crew chief.

She glanced at the row of quivering instruments dotted across the utilitarian dashboard.

Oil and water temperatures. Good.

Oil and fuel pressures. Check.

Volt gauge. On the mark.

But there was no fuel gauge. Gassing up was an art, not a science. Timing was everything. She'd run forty laps since her last pit stop and was now approaching the midway mark in the five-hundred-mile race, so far without a major calamity. The Number 127 car had blown a tire a half hour ago, but he'd been at the end of the pack and had managed to pull off safely without the caution flag having to be raised.

Come on, someone, screw up.

She just needed a minor mishap. A shredded tire in the pack behind her. An oil spill. Enough of a hazard to bring out the yellow caution flag so she could make a pit stop while the field was frozen in slow motion. That way she'd stand a better chance of not losing her position.

"I'm good for one more lap," she answered into her mike.

"*Now,* Gabby," another male voice commanded.

For a moment his tone reminded her of her mother, and in that split second she was tempted to go into defiance mode and make another circuit to spite him. But Vaughn Steiner was definitely not Della O'Farrell. Not even close. He was the person in charge, though. The team owner. The guy who paid the bills and made all this possible. Besides, he was a former driver. She trusted his instincts. Other owners watched from a distance. Vaughn liked to still be in the action.

She snapped the wheel to the left onto the entrance to pit road, lined her vehicle up precisely and tapped the brakes.

Ahead on her left she saw her red-and-black team logo and the metal sign with her car number, 111, bobbing up and down atop a pole. She headed for the stall, clearly outlined on the pavement in yellow, worked the brake pedal with her left foot and listened to the countdown. She had to be completely inside the box. Those were the rules, and there were plenty of them.

Five, four, three, two, one.

Even before she'd come to a complete stop, her team was leaping over the infield's low concrete wall and surrounding her sleek black vehicle festooned with colorful decals. The most prominent, the big one on the hood, was OI, O'Farrell Industries, the local family business her father had brought from near bankruptcy to become a national trademark.

The engine still rumbling, the right side of the vehicle tilted sharply up. The whir of an air wrench removed lug nuts while behind her on the left specially blended high-octane gasoline streamed into her fuel cell from two 11-gallon cans held high aloft.

The sharp, pungent smells of hot asphalt, burned rubber, raw fuel and lubricants were better than an aphrodisiac. No high could compare with this.

A water bottle attached to a long pole poked in through the net covering the window opening. She grabbed the plastic straw and sucked the ice water into her parched mouth. Even with the cooling system she must already have sweated a gallon in the stifling car. But her mind wasn't on the 120-degree heat or the perspiration leeching out of every pore of her body or the claustrophobic snugness of her seat and harness. Her thoughts were focused on only one thing. The race. Nothing else mattered.

The right side of the car bounced down. Two tires changed. A second later the left side angled up. Two to go. The seven-man team moved with quick, sure, practiced efficiency.

"You're hanging back too long on the turn before accelerating into the backstretch," Vaughn told her, his voice coming through the radio headset. It was the only way to communicate in the deafening roar around them: the howl of unmuffled, high-performance engines streaking by, the crowd in the grandstands across the black-ribboned road cheering wildly, the PA system blaring overhead.

"Gotcha," she replied, and instinctively nodded, making her aware of the weight of her helmet. She swallowed one last desperate sip of water while fighting a tight grin at the irony of the advice. Vaughn usually told her to back off, to not be so aggressive. Apparently his counsel had overcome her lead-footed impulses.

Easy fix, she vowed. Easy fix.

The left side of the car bounced onto the pavement.

"Go. Go. Go. Go. Go."

Gabby spurted forward, burning rubber, to make up every precious second. The stop to change four tires and fill her tank had lasted less than fourteen seconds. The streamlined car, theoretically a stock Ford Fusion, had no speedometer. She monitored the tachometer instead to keep under the 55 mph speed limit on pit road. Exceeding it would mean a serious penalty. Safety came first in this high-energy, inherently dangerous sport. She hit the track and revved the 750 horsepower, custom-built engine to full throttle and experienced that exhilarating surge of adrenaline race drivers thrive on. Junkies, all of them, for speed.

She zoomed onto the stretch, her foot rammed to the floorboard. One hundred forty miles an hour. One sixty. One eighty. The high-powered engine screamed. Her gloved hands sweat. Turn One was coming up. Jem Nordstrom's Chevy Monte Carlo roared beside her on the right, trying to inch ahead in tiny spurts. Freddie Harris was edging his Dodge Charger up in her left rear quadrant. No way would she allow him in.

She'd taken first once in the NASCAR Busch Series—

what a blast that had been—but this was the NASCAR NEXTEL Cup Series. It didn't get any better than this.

Jem and Freddie were now a lap ahead of her, but they were heading for pit stops. If she could hold her own on this lap she had a shot for the lead and, if she could maintain it, Victory Lane.

Decision time came again. Should she slow down enough to hug the inside of the curve, and probably be overtaken on the outside in the backstretch by Jem, returning after his pit stop? Or keep up speed a little longer and take the curve wide, forcing him to slip behind her rather than widen his turning radius? The problem was that it would leave her vulnerable to a slingshot maneuver on the inside by Freddie, who was also back on the track.

Choices. Tactics. Wits. God, she loved this.

Be aggressive, Vaughn had coached her. Don't hold back on the turn. Got it.

Gabby maintained her speed, nudging two hundred miles per hour now, and hugged the inside lane—until the seat of her pants told her she was about to lose traction. Oh, so reluctantly, she eased up on the gas, just enough to maintain control. Halfway through the second part of the turn she flattened the pedal to the firewall. The new wide, treadless rear tires fishtailed for a split second before they grabbed the hot, tacky asphalt and shot down the straightaway. Freddie and Jem, still on her tail, hung close, but Gabby still owned the lead.

A broad grin had her cheeks touching the padded sides of her helmet. Mustn't gloat, she chided herself, and grinned some more.

Jem's car nosed forward, ahead of Freddie's, and shifted left to the inside. He was trying to coax Gabby to the right so he could gain the inside lane, the shortest circumference of any circle.

"Bite me," she whispered.

The next turn loomed. Don't panic and don't yield. If he wanted to play chicken, she'd show him.

She pushed a little longer this time, ran wide-open before letting up marginally on the gas. Jem's Chevy began to drift a little more to the left. No, damn it, she wouldn't give him the inside of the curve, the lead. No way.

The tight radius had her rear end starting to break to the right. Instinctively she countersteered—which took her still farther to the right.

Jem sling-shotted ahead from the inside lane. The radius of the turn tightened. Gabby refused to lighten up on the gas pedal.

But *he* did. Damn it.

Her left front fender caught his right rear. All of a sudden his tail began to break. Centrifugal force took over. There was no way around him. The chain reaction commenced. She T-boned him. Then Freddie clipped her.

Gabby sat helpless as her Ford began a slow, counterclockwise rotation across the steeply banked track in a blue-gray cloud of acrid smoke.

She muttered a curse. The shriek of tires and the stench of burning rubber filled her nostrils. Her heart pounded like a pile driver as she gripped the steering wheel.

Jem's Monte Carlo paralleled her motion. For a breathtaking moment they whirled like synchronized dancers. Then came the inevitable, nerve-shattering crunch of metal.

Jem bounced off the outside wall. Gabby struck him sideways on the rebound and ricocheted in front of Freddie. He swerved, but not fast enough. He rammed into her again. Bumper cars without the laughter. The siren call of race cars roared past them. Gabby's ears buzzed. Her body lurched from side to side against the seat harness.

And her heart sank into her stomach. For Gabby O'Farrell, this race was over.

CHAPTER TWO

FISTS CLENCHED, jaw locked, Vaughn Steiner watched the whole episode from atop the hauler in the infield. Nothing he hadn't seen hundreds of times before and experienced dozens of times himself when he was a driver. Yet his heart was pounding like a rookie's when Gabby lost control and went into a slow, spellbinding rotation, like the final revolution in a taunting game of spin the bottle. He'd lived with danger, thrived on it all his life. Yet standing by, observing this relatively innocuous crash, scared the hell out of him.

His fear was all out of proportion. He knew that. Gabby wasn't in serious danger. The cars behind her, driven by experts, were able to give her a wide berth. There was no further chain reaction. No one rolled. No one flipped. There was no pileup.

He took a series of deep breaths and willed his heartbeat to slow down.

His precious Number 111 car was a mess, of course, and out of commission for the rest of this race. Gabby had been slammed hard, but the carefully engineered rolled-steel cage she sat in protected her. The biggest threat in crashes was fire. In this case there hadn't been any. Yet he'd felt unbearable anxiety for her safety and an unrealistic desire to snatch her out of harm's way. This uncharacteristic reaction left him feeling helpless and that made him angry.

While Mack Roberts, the crew chief who had been with him for nearly ten years, scrambled his team to recover the car, and the track crew drove Gabby to the infield care center, Vaughn paced back and forth.

His anger was fully justified, he told himself. She'd blown the race, wrecked his car. Cost him time and a lot of money. Damn it all. He had every right to be pissed.

He had to remind himself that his other car on the track, driven by Brett Conroe, was near the back of the first pack, in nineteenth place. Okay, could be better, but at least he was still in the race. There was plenty of time for him to move up. Vaughn had few illusions that Brett would win, but the guy was at least making a good showing. Focus on the positive, Vaughn told himself. Focus on the positive.

Yet all he could think about was Gabby.

He must have been crazy to take on a woman driver. What the hell had he been thinking? He wouldn't be fretting this way if it was a man behind the wheel.

He was waiting for her when a truck dropped her off in the garage area. He already knew from a walkie-talkie report that she was all right. The medics had checked her over for broken bones and for any cuts or lacerations that might need attention. No treatment required. She'd be sore as hell tomorrow, though, from the hard slamming she'd received. Vaughn could promise her that. He also knew from years of experience on the track that the biggest bruise she'd have would be the self-imposed one on her ass from kicking herself.

On a deep sigh of frustration he decided he better not think about that or any other part of her all too feminine anatomy.

He kept his right hand tucked in his red-and-black team jacket pocket as he strode toward her. He needed another pill, damn it, but it would have to wait. Somehow, at the moment, the pain felt right, gave him an edge.

"You blew it," he said when she came to within a few feet of him.

He didn't raise his voice. He didn't shout. He didn't peal into a stream of epithets and insults. That wasn't his style. People who worked with him for any length of time learned soon enough that when he lowered his voice he was seething and when it got down to a whisper he was at his most furious. He wasn't at that stage yet, but he was damn close.

He could see by the way she refused to look at him directly that her instinct was to say she was sorry, but she didn't. That pleased him. He didn't want apologies or excuses. Torqued as he was, he still found himself having to suppress an urge to put his arms around her, to console the hurt little girl he saw in her eyes. Except she wasn't a little girl, and he wasn't her father.

Blue eyes. Sometimes they were as bright and clear as the summer sky. Right now they were dark and troubled. Angry, too. Not at his juvenile sarcasm. At herself. Good. She needed to engage that passion, channel it, harness its power. Gabby O'Farrell was a better driver than even she realized. She had the instincts, but she still had to find her confidence zone.

"You told me to be aggressive." She threw the words back at him, recovering her pride.

"Aggressive," he countered, "doesn't mean stupid, Gabby. You were in third place with a hundred laps to go. Why'd you have to push it?"

"Because I had a chance at second," she snapped, her voice only marginally below shrill. "Maybe even first."

"It was too early. You were being greedy."

Beyond them the zoom and howl of cars streaking by was mere background noise to the energy throbbing between them. Mechanics and other crew members were standing around, keeping their distance but still straining to hear what they could.

"You should have bided your time. Instead you let emotions fog your judgment. You threw away all the hard work of everyone on this team, Gabby!"

The weight of the accusation slumped her shoulders. Catching herself, she straightened. "That's not fair."

"No? Who was driving the car?"

"Jem was pushing—" she started.

"Of course he was pushing. He's out there to win, not escort you around the track. Your job is to outsmart him, not allow him to goad you into making stupid mistakes. You could have held your space and challenged him on the straightaway, lined yourself up for a better position in the next turn."

Vaughn shook his head, his eyes never leaving her.

"This isn't the Busch Series, Gabby," he went on. "The tactics you used there don't apply here. I thought you understood that. I guess I was wrong."

He finally broke contact and headed toward the soda machine at the other end of the bay. He was thirsty and he really needed to take that pain pill.

GABBY KNEW EXACTLY what he was referring to. The bump-draft. It was used in the NASCAR Busch Series all the time.

If you got right up behind a car, the two of you shared a single tunnel of air. It was called drafting and allowed both of you together to go faster than either of you could normally go on your own. The lead car was at a disadvantage, however. Drafting disabled the spoiler on its trunk lid, which was designed to put downward pressure on the back tires, improving their traction. By incapacitating the spoiler, the tail end became loose, light. All it took was a bump to destabilize it. At slower NASCAR Busch Series speeds, the break was controllable. At NASCAR NEXTEL speeds, averaging 180 mph, it could be disastrous. Like today.

The irony was that she'd had no intention of touching the Chevy, just getting close enough to disturb the airflow over his spoiler, lifting his rear end enough for the centrifugal force of the turn to naturally carry him to the right enough to let her in. If Jem hadn't slowed down…

As much as she wanted to argue the point with Vaughn, she knew she was in a no-win situation. Engaging in a shouting match with her owner—assuming she could even get him to raise his voice—would only make her look weak. For now she had no choice but to endure his tongue-lashing. Later, after they'd reviewed the tapes and gone over every second of what had happened, after they'd studied it all in slow motion, maybe he'd see it hadn't been entirely her fault.

But would he? All Jem had done was let up on the gas. Even if he'd mashed the brake pedal, it wouldn't have been obvious. There were no brake lights on stock cars. What looked like head and taillights were nothing more than decals.

Vaughn was right. She'd been the one in the driver's seat. She'd been the one behind Jem.

She was giving herself a good, hard, mental kick in the butt when she sensed the tension around her shift. She turned to see Jem Nordstrom stomping down the row of open garages toward her, a small media entourage in his wake.

Oh, great. Now I'm going to get it from him, too.

Nordstrom had never made any secret of his disdain for "girl" drivers in his manly world of powerful machines.

"You stupid little bit—" He caught himself, swallowed the last syllable. Bitch wasn't a four-letter word, but under the circumstances it might be regarded as close enough.

"Back off," Vaughn ordered, reversing course and heading toward them. She imagined his arm protectively encircling her and felt a strange warm comfort in his closeness.

"Screw you, Steiner," Jem snarled. "I just lost this friggin' race because of her stupid incompetence."

A crowd of people with garage passes was closing in behind the reporters. Cameras clicked and camcorders whirred.

"Watch your language, Nordstrom," Vaughn warned, "if you don't want to get slapped with a great big fine."

NASCAR prided itself on being a family spectator sport. Its members had to adhere to certain rules. One of them was a strict prohibition against profane language. The standard was simple. If you wouldn't say it in front of your kids, you didn't say it at all, at least not where microphones could pick it up.

"And don't blame other people for your own inadequacies."

"My inadequacies? I've been racing at this track for thirteen years. How long has this powder puff been tooling around any speedway? Two weeks?"

"If you're so experienced," Vaughn challenged, his voice raised enough for everyone to hear, "how come you let yourself get spun out by the vehicle behind you. That's amateur stuff, Nordstrom. You should know better."

"I should..." he sputtered, his ruddy face growing redder.

"That's bull—" Again he caught himself in time to bite off the offending last syllable. "Don't lay that crap on me."

Gabby could feel the people around them soaking in the drama, made all the more threatening by Jem's ham-hock fists held rigid at his sides. In spite of all the testosterone that permeated the sport, actual physical violence was rare. There was occasional posturing, of course, like what Jem was doing now, but he knew if he took a swing—whether it connected or not—his racing season could be over. Not to mention the disgrace of having attacked a man with a disability.

"You were the one who backed off on the turn, Nordstrom. What's the matter, afraid of a little speed?"

Gabby's jaw dropped. So Vaughn did know. She should have realized he would. Didn't keep him from giving her a hard time, though, she thought.

She almost laughed at the stunned expression on Jem's face. "You don't know what you're talking about." He grumbled, but the statement lacked certitude. "I didn't slow."

"Yes, you did," Vaughn stated with utter conviction.

"You calling me a liar?"

"You always back off early going into a turn," Vaughn persisted.

For a split second Jem's face went blank. He seemed as shocked by the accusation as offended by it. His gaze dropped to the pill bottle in Vaughn's right hand. Looking suddenly smug, he leaned closer to Vaughn and muttered, "You're pitiful, Steiner. You know that?"

Vaughn's color darkened and his jaw clenched. His left hand curled into a hard fist, while his right hand slid back into his pocket.

Pleased with the reaction, Jem sneered and retreated a step.

"Of course you defend her," he said loud enough for the crowd around them to hear. "What choice do you have? She's your meal ticket."

He shook his head in mocking sympathy. "It's all very sad, isn't it, folks?" he said to the people around him. "Seems like the only thing Vaughn Steiner, the great two-time NASCAR NEXTEL Cup Champion, is good for anymore is teaching little girls how to Sunday drive."

CHAPTER THREE

THERE WAS NO NEED for an owner to stick around after a race when neither of his cars were winners. The crew chiefs were responsible for clearing out the pits and garage areas, for getting the cars loaded into the haulers and on the road back home to Charlotte or their next destination, in this case, Las Vegas. Vaughn had a private jet standing by at the airport, ready to fly him home to North Carolina. Yet he felt as though he'd be running away if he left now.

He knew he shouldn't let Jem's parting shot bother him, but it rankled nevertheless. He did his best to disguise the loss of function in his right hand and arm, and for the most part he thought he pulled it off rather well. The last thing he wanted was to be pitied, but Jem had gone beyond that; he'd mocked him for his weakness, as if Vaughn were himself responsible for his handicap, or even worse, faking it.

The day hadn't been a complete loss, Vaughn consoled himself. Brett Conroe had come in eighth, earning one hundred and forty-two points, as well as a thousand-dollar bonus offered by one of the sponsors for finishing in the top ten. Gabby's elimination had set her back in points, but it didn't mean she was out of consideration for the season's NASCAR NEXTEL Cup, only that she would have to work harder to catch up.

It all came down to points. It wasn't unusual for a driver to qualify for the final series of competitions—the Chase for the NASCAR NEXTEL Cup—without winning a single preliminary race. He simply had to accumulate enough points overall to be among the final top ten contenders or get within four hundred points of the top ten. But winning sure helped.

Conroe was good, no question about that, and he definitely had the potential to do better, but despite his flashy personal appeal to the fans, he was a relatively conservative driver. That wasn't entirely bad. Perseverance and consistency often trumped daring bursts of energy. Deep down inside, however, Vaughn didn't feel the same level of excitement about Conroe as he did with Gabby—as a driver.

Gabby... Well, Gabby had the potential for one of those dazzling careers that legends were made of, the kind Vaughn, himself, had once had.

Inside the hauler's lounge, he grabbed a soft drink from the refrigerator and finally washed down the pill he should have taken more than an hour earlier.

He was going to pay for the delay. Already the burning sensation in his right arm was intense, which meant the medication would take longer to kick in and be less effective when it finally did. He could take two tablets, but as usual he decided to tough it out. He hated having to pop pills to begin with and the last thing he wanted was to become any more dependent on them than he already was. He could handle a little pain—or a lot, if he had to.

The worse part was the uncertainty. The doctors he'd conferred with couldn't even decide what to label his condition. Some called it RSDS—Reflex Sympathetic Dystrophy Syndrome. Others used the term CRPS—Complex

Regional Pain Syndrome. They did agree it was probably a neurological disorder precipitated by the shoulder dislocation he'd suffered two years ago, but they couldn't make up their minds about the prognosis or treatment. Not only was he in nearly constant pain at some level, but he was losing strength and dexterity. Or had been. He'd recently begun a new round of physical therapy to counteract the threat of muscle and skeletal atrophy, and he felt it was helping—sometimes. Or maybe it was just wishful thinking because the thought of losing all use of the limb was even more depressing than the actual pain.

Back outside he sipped the cola and watched the Number 111 car being loaded into the overhead compartment of the hauler, above the meticulously neat workshop. It felt so unnatural to be standing here, doing nothing. A spectator. Useless. Each member of the team had an assigned task and each pursued it with single-minded dedication. Except him. He just watched.

If the car was salvageable, they'd have parts shipped directly to the track. With this rare two-week break between races, the car might be ready for Vegas. Chances were, though, that Gabby would be driving the backup.

Surveying the busy scene, Vaughn's attention was inevitably drawn to Gabby herself as she talked to members of the crew. He couldn't help admire the way she filled out her fitted uniform. The long sweeping curve of her hips. The swell of her breasts. She kept her dark hair short. Normally it crowned her head in natural unaffected waves. Right now it was half plastered, half curly from her sweaty helmet. She'd run her fingers through it to set it free, but not to groom it. There was something endearing about the fact that she didn't preen.

He didn't have to hear her words to know she was thanking the guys for their help and probably apologizing for not doing better.

They'd voiced doubts when Vaughn first announced who their driver would be. That was to be expected. She wasn't completely new to NASCAR, but she was to the NASCAR NEXTEL Series, and while her record in the NASCAR Busch Series was good, it was hardly exceptional or very extensive. One win. Two seconds. Four thirds. Half a dozen eliminations. And a slew of intermediate finishes.

And, of course, she was a woman. That alone made her stand out. There hadn't been many women drivers in the nearly sixty years since NASCAR had been founded and none of them had won the Championship at the end of the season. By and large they hadn't done badly, either. Maybe, Vaughn had reminded them, Gabby O'Farrell would be the one to break the record and bring home the Championship. He'd seen doubt on their faces, but they'd agreed to give her a chance to prove herself.

Unfortunately today hadn't been to her credit.

"HAVE TO REPLACE a bunch of panels," Larry Mason, one of the general mechanics, told Gabby. "So what else is new? The real question is whether the frame is bent."

"We'll definitely need to replace the front sway bar, the track bar and both shocks on the left," Jimmy Cranford, his cohort, contributed. "Brake rotors on the left are gone, but—" he shrugged "—I've seen worse."

Steam had been billowing from under the hood when Gabby finally came to rest after pirouetting across the raceway. She'd flipped off the ignition toggle switch—there was no key—but by then the damage might already have been done.

"What about the engine?" she asked. A new one cost about eighty thousand dollars, almost half the price of the entire car.

"Can't tell for sure," Mike Tackett, the engine specialist said. "We'll know if the block's cracked when we check it out in Vegas."

They carried an extra in the hauler for just this kind of contingency. Trading them out would only take a few hours. Then would come all the test runs and fine tuning. Every car was custom-built; every combination of components unique in their performance.

"Thanks, guys, for everything. I mean it. You've been great. I'm sorry I let you down today."

"Crap," Larry said. "You heard Steiner. Nordstrom was the real problem. He's been out for Vaughn's blood for years. You just happened to be a convenient proxy today."

She was still glowing from Vaughn's defense. Okay, any good crew chief or owner would do the same, defend his people against outsiders, but the fact that he'd seen and understood exactly what had happened was reassuring—and a little scary. She'd never be able to bluff Vaughn Steiner, that was for sure. Not that she had any plans to. She was glad, though, that she hadn't gotten a chance to explain what had happened. It would have sounded like an excuse. This had been better. She knew now that as a former driver he understood intuitively what had gone wrong.

"Thanks again, guys. I'll see y'all in Vegas a week from Thursday," she called as they dispersed to their jobs.

She turned and was about to walk down the line to her coach when Brett Conroe came around the back of his hauler, spied her and sidled up alongside.

"Tough break out there today," he said, walking beside her.

He was trying to sound sympathetic, but she wasn't fooled. Last week at Daytona he'd started in fourteenth position and ended up in thirty-ninth. Today he'd moved up from seventeenth to eighth. So now he was gloating. Okay, she decided, he had a right to.

Six foot one, with curly brown hair, a golden California tan, medium blue eyes, perfect white teeth and still a bachelor at twenty-nine, he was on the Most Wanted list of a lot of NASCAR's female fans.

"Congratulations on your eighth place," Gabby said.

"Actually I was hoping for higher, but it's still early in the season." They stopped and he moved a little too close, invading her personal space.

"Look," he said, "traffic to the airport is going to be brutal for the next couple of hours. Why don't we go over to my coach? I have a casserole one of my fans brought me. I can stick it in the oven while we knock back a beer. Or sip some wine if you prefer. I've got TiVo. We can watch today's race together. Maybe I can give you a few pointers on how to avoid being disqualified next time."

Gabby resisted the urge to stomp on his foot, then kick him in the shin.

"Gee, thanks, Brett," she said sweetly, "but I have to wash my hair."

He put his arm around her shoulder, squeezed. "Don't you worry about your hair, baby. My shower is big enough for both of us. I'll be glad to work in the shampoo and give you a nice stimulating massage."

Golly, was she supposed to melt at the invitation?

"Thanks, but no thanks, Brett. Now, please let me go."

She started to step out of his clutches, but instead of

taking the hint and releasing her, he tightened his embrace, and for a second she felt the stirrings of panic. The guy was big. He was strong. And he apparently wasn't used to taking no for an answer. She placed a palm firmly on the side of his rib cage to push him away. Her next self-defense Tae Kwon Do maneuver would leave him on the ground groaning, but she'd really prefer to avoid that if she could.

"Conroe, back off. Now," came a voice.

Automatically, Brett shifted around, unconsciously dragging Gabby with him but also giving her a view of the man behind them. Vaughn Steiner was standing on the top step of the hauler.

Brett gazed up at him for a moment, then raised his hands. "Hey, just a little misunderstanding," he told his boss. Taking a small step to the side, he smiled over at Gabby. "Sorry if I misread your signals."

Gabby glared at him. There hadn't been any signals and he knew it. She just hoped Vaughn did.

"Gabby," Vaughn said, without looking at her, "I'm sure you have things to do. We'll go over today's race when I see you in Vegas. Then we can work on a strategy for that track." His tone was all business—and dismissive. To Brett he said, "Come with me."

WITHOUT SPARING GABBY a glance or waiting for a response from Brett, Vaughn retreated into the hauler, striding down the narrow corridor formed by the tool bins that lined both sides of the eighteen-wheeler, toward the lounge at the front end. Two members of Conroe's team were there grumbling insults at the competition as they watched a replay of the day's race on the TV monitor mounted high up on the wall. One glanced over, saw the expression on Vaughn's face, rose from the edge of the seat and quickly dropped the remote on the leather cushion beside him.

"Let's go see if we can help the others load up," he said to his companion, who also jumped to his feet. They mumbled inarticulate phrases, squeezed past the two men and darted through the narrow doorway.

Vaughn did an about-face and confronted the young driver. "Do you know what sexual harassment is?"

"Come on, boss," Brett responded, all boyish innocence. "I wasn't harassing anyone."

"You came mighty close. When Gabby said no, the conversation, and especially the physical contact, should have ended then and there."

"She's a big girl. She can take care of herself."

"You're right, and after she gave you a good swift kick in the family jewels she would have yelled harassment and your ass would be hurting even more than your private parts."

The graphic language, unusual for Vaughn Steiner, momentarily widened Conroe's eyes. "You're blowing this all out of proportion," he finally replied. "Why don't you just mind your own business?"

Vaughn tucked his aching right hand under his left bicep and crossed his arms. "Let's get a few things straight, Conroe. As long as you're driving one of my cars, you will conduct yourself in a professional manner at all times, on and off the track. If you don't, you will no longer be a member of this team. I really don't give a damn about your personal life—as long as it doesn't interfere with the job, the morale of the people you work with or the NASCAR image. If, on the other hand, Gabby O'Farrell or any other woman says no, your advances stop immediately. Have I made myself clear?"

Conroe shifted his jaw. "You're not my father, Steiner, and I'm over eighteen. So stay out of my face." He shifted his weight to one hip. "You're not fooling anybody, you know. Everyone can see the way you look at her. You'd like a piece of that action yourself."

Vaughn took a slow, deep breath while he considered the man in front of him very carefully. After a long pause he said in a voice so soft Conroe probably had to lip read to hear him.

"You're on the edge, Conroe. If you want to continue to be a member of Steiner Racing you'd better watch your mouth and your actions. You're right. I'm not your father, but don't ever speak to me in that tone and don't ever make me address this issue with you again. If you do, I assure you there won't be any discussion and the meeting won't last but a few seconds, which is all I'll need to send you packing. Now get out of here."

Conroe clearly wanted to say something in reply but wisely chose not to. Instead, he turned on his heel and left the van.

CHAPTER FOUR

IT WAS AFTER TWO in the morning by the time Gabby finally turned the key in the lock to her condo in Greensboro, entered and turned off the security alarm. The day that had started out with such high hopes was certainly ending differently.

Her mind kept reliving the race, particularly its last few minutes. Logic told her it was over. In the past. Unchangeable. Learn from it and move on. That was the sensible thing to do, except she couldn't seem to escape the hurt expression in Vaughn's chocolate-brown eyes when Jem Nordstrom hurled his insults at him. Damn it. Jem would never have had a chance to say those horrible things if she hadn't screwed up and given him the opening.

Her best recourse now was to make Jem eat his words by chalking up more points than he did and the best way to do that was to win as many races as possible. Over the next eight months she'd be competing in another twenty-four races scattered across the country, one nearly every weekend. If at the end of that round she made the cut for the Chase, the NASCAR World Series, she'd be in ten more races, most of them in the southeast, culminating in the award of the NASCAR NEXTEL Cup. Vaughn had taken the Cup twice in a row. Jem never had. Wouldn't it be sweet to be the first woman to win it?

Maybe it was an unrealistic expectation in her rookie season, but as her father had reminded her many times, *If you don't try, you'll never succeed and you'll never know if you could have done it. Be bold.*

She went directly to the kitchen for a container of yogurt to settle her stomach before turning in. The steward in the first-class section of her flight home had served poached salmon, rice pilaf, a Caesar salad and a piece of cheesecake for dessert, but that had been hours ago. Right now she didn't feel hungry as much as hollow.

The light on the answering machine on the counter was blinking.

She was tempted to ignore it, to change into her baggy flannel PJs and crawl into bed. Not only was she physically and emotionally exhausted, her body was sore and achy from today's wreck. If she went to bed right away and fell instantly asleep, she might get four hours' rest. Twenty-four didn't feel as if it would be enough. But she'd grown up compulsive as well as impulsive and the idea of leaving a message unlistened to was about as likely as pulling to the right in a turn to let someone pass her on the inside.

She pressed the play button.

The first message was from Glenna Holbrook, her public relations manager, reminding her of her ten o'clock appearance to sign autographs tomorrow—this morning now—at an auto-parts store in Fayetteville, outside Ft. Bragg. She always received an enthusiastic reception from the troops and their families. She'd wear her driver's uniform, of course, complete with helmet. Kids loved putting it on, then shouting "Vroom, vroom."

The second message was also from Glenna, this time relaying a request from a bookstore in Sanford for her to come in at her convenience to sign a few books about NASCAR, even though she hadn't written them and wasn't even mentioned in them. Glenna suggested she stop by there on her way back from Fayetteville, since it was on the way. Gabby decided to coordinate the time in the morning.

She clicked the button to play the third message.

"Hello, dear, this is your mother."

Gabby wished now she hadn't worried about the darn answering machine. Telephone calls from her mother always seemed to presage trouble.

"I just wanted to let you know that I've accepted a dinner invitation for the two of us for tomorrow evening. You did tell me you'd be home on Monday, didn't you? I do wish you had a regular job like other people, Gabriella. It's so hard keeping track of where you are. Anyway, it's at eight o'clock at the Davids'. You remember Reggie. He's the CEO of Emporico. He and your father used to play golf together. That was years ago, of course. Just a small, informal get-together. Marjorie says there'll only be ten or twelve of us. I thought you might wear that lavender dress I gave you for your birthday, since I've never seen you wear it. Your pearls would be perfect with it, but I'm sure you'll decide for yourself what you want to wear. You always do. But please, dear, make it something feminine, not like that horrible pants outfit you wore at the Robins' last month. You could have been mistaken for a field marshal." Della hadn't liked the epaulets on the jacket. "It really was quite unsuitable. Oh, and before this tape runs out on me, the address is…"

Gabby copied it down on the notepad by the phone. She didn't want to have to listen to her mother again.

The last message was from Marjorie David herself.

"Gabriella, darling, your mother gave me your number. I'm so pleased you'll be able to join us tomorrow evening. It's been ages, much too long. Della also mentioned that you'll be out all day tomorrow running from one appointment to another."

So Mom did keep up with her schedule. Why did she think it necessary to disguise the fact? Oh, well. Can't change Mom.

"So you'll no doubt be rushed for time. And you probably have no idea how to find our place. Well, not to worry, my dear. I talked to my son this afternoon and mentioned you would be joining us. Trey's terribly excited about seeing you again and he offered to pick you up, since he lives right there in Greensboro and insists he has to return home after dinner. Heaven knows why. Anyway, there's no point in both of you making the trip separately. Traveling is so much more pleasant when you have company, don't you think? Your mother gave me your address and I passed it on to him. Della was sure you wouldn't mind. Trey said he'll be by to get you at six-thirty, if that's all right. I know you're frightfully busy, my dear. How exciting it must be to drive race cars. I can't wait to hear all about it."

Not if Mom can help it, Gabby thought.

"Trey's cell phone number in case you have to get hold of him…"

Gabby copied it down, too.

"Well," she muttered out loud as she poked her head inside the refrigerator and pulled out a container of strawberry-banana yogurt, "I know what the agenda is for tomorrow night."

Gabby had met the Davids at several social functions her mother had dragged her to over the past few years. Since "Reggie" was Reginald David Jr., she supposed Trey was the nickname for Reginald David the Third, but she couldn't remember ever meeting him. Yet his mother said he was excited about meeting her *again.* If they had met before, it definitely couldn't have been recently.

Oh, no. Was he that nerdy-looking kid with the acne and dirty glasses she'd met at some wedding or birthday party back when she was—what?—thirteen. He'd been a year or so older. All he did was stammer while he talked to her breasts. Granted, she was exceptionally well-developed for her age, but that was no excuse. She shook her head. As if boys ever needed an excuse to stare at girls' boobs. Jerk.

Gabby chuckled, tossed the empty container in the trash, put the spoon in the sink, set the security system for the night and made her way to the bedroom humming "Matchmaker, Matchmaker." Five minutes later she crawled into her queen-sized bed and turned out the light.

Reginald David the Third. Wonderful.

Ever since her father's death last year, her mother had had three goals. The first was to lure Gabby away from auto racing. Della had never been happy with her daughter driving "those gaudy, noisy cars," but she'd kept her disapproval in check while her dad, Brock, was alive. With his health deteriorating, Gabby could see she hadn't wanted to upset him. She also knew that despite his illness her mother couldn't win in a battle of wills with him.

Now that he was gone, though, Della made no attempt to hide her loathing for Gabby's choice of lifestyle. "Too bad," Gabby mumbled as she fluffed up her pillow. She wasn't about to abandon it just because her mother didn't think it was "ladylike."

Della's second goal wasn't really new—to marry her daughter off to a man of substance and social position.

Gabby took a deep breath and gave her pillow a punch. That campaign had been under way since she was seventeen, and dear Mom was no closer to success now than she had been then. It wasn't that Gabby didn't like men. Or that she wasn't interested in marriage and family. Just not yet. For one thing, she hadn't met the man of her dreams. Plus, her focus was on racing stock cars.

Trey David would certainly fit very nicely into her mother's plan. Emporico was one of the largest retailers in the country and was starting to expand overseas. The Davids were reputedly worth not millions but billions.

The third goal, now that Della had taken over as head of O'Farrell Industries, was to increase company profits through safe, conservative management. As far as Gabby could tell from glancing at the myriad corporate reports she received as a member of the board, her mother wasn't doing any better on that score than she was on the others. Of course, Gabby hadn't attended a meeting in months, so the figures could be misleading. All Gabby was really interested in was that OI continued to be her NASCAR sponsor. Ten million dollars this year so far.

Hmm. Could Della have a fourth goal in mind? A corporate alliance between O'Farrell Industries and Emporico? It would certainly be very profitable for OI, since it would reduce, maybe even eliminate, their need for individual store outlets. Surely her mother wasn't using Gabby as a business tool. She wouldn't sink that low… Would she? Of course not. But if Trey and Gabby just happened to hit it off…

She gave her pillow another quick punch and tried to picture the scrawny kid of fifteen years ago. It was hard because she hadn't paid much attention to him back then. He'd been an inch or two shorter, as she recalled. Gangly. All elbows and angles. And definitely lacking in social finesse. Did he still stammer?

She attempted to age him in her overtired mind, but for some crazy reason her brain kept confusing him with Vaughn Steiner. Which really didn't make sense. The kid she remembered, if it was the right one, had been towheaded. Vaughn had black hair. The gawking adolescent had had blue eyes, or maybe they were hazel. Didn't matter. Vaughn's eyes were unmistakably brown, basset-hound brown, although sometimes they became almost black, like today when he'd been so steaming mad at Conroe for trying to put the make on her. She could have handled the situation on her own and she probably ought to be offended that he thought she needed rescuing, but it was sort of nice to know he was looking out for her. She smiled to herself. Her protector. Her chivalrous knight. Even if he was her boss.

Gabby snuggled deeper into the pillow and tried to imagine how those dark, mysterious eyes might gaze at her if she'd won the race... How would they look at her *when* she won a race...

CHAPTER FIVE

"Coming," Gabby called out at 6:35 p.m. the following evening as she strode toward the door in answer to the bell.

She was wearing the lavender dress her mother had given her and the pearls that had been a present from her father on her sixteenth birthday, at what her mother insisted on calling her "coming-out" party. It all felt too girly to her now. She was much more comfortable these days in jeans and a cotton shirt or, if she was dressing up, a pantsuit and blouse, but she'd learned a long time ago to go along with her mother's wishes on minor things like clothes. There were plenty of bigger issues to get into contests over, such as where she lived and how she spent her time. And they did, regularly.

Gabby swung the door open and was about to say, "You're late," but the accusation stalled before she could utter a sound. It took a moment for her eyes to work their way up the wall standing in front of her. Oh, momma. This guy didn't look anything like the pimply faced kid she thought she remembered from fifteen years ago. Didn't look anything like Vaughn Steiner, either, for that matter. This hunk stood at least six foot two, had a lusciously smooth tanned complexion with nary a hint of teenage acne. Honey-blond hair, sea-green eyes and lashes long enough to make a girl weep.

"Gabby? Hi. I'm Trey. Sorry I'm late, but I—"

"You're not really." What's a mere five minutes? she decided. Inconsequential. And the wait was worth it. Oh, yeah. Definitely worth it. "Come in."

She closed the door behind him and let her eyes feast on the way his custom-tailored, fawn-colored suit jacket draped his broad shoulders and narrowed down to slender hips. My, my.

Impressive. Yes, indeedy. Very impressive.

But why was this guy still available? He should have been snatched up long ago. Or maybe he was married after all, and his wife was home with sick kids or out of town visiting her folks or away on business. No, she didn't believe any of it and a quick glance confirmed that he wasn't wearing a wedding ring. Of course, he could be divorced.

"I just need to get my purse."

She proceeded to her bedroom, very aware of his eyes following her, grabbed her small evening bag from the top of the dresser and returned to the living room. He was examining titles in the bookcase.

"You still play?" he asked, motioning toward the grand piano a few feet away.

"Not very often these days."

"I heard you play once. My mother set me up on a blind date with a girl from Bryn Mawr, so I got to hear you give a performance at your alma mater. Rachmaninoff. You were good."

That took her by surprise. Her flirtation with a musical career had lasted only a year. She'd been good but not great, and the numbing hours of practice it would have taken to become great had held no appeal whatsoever. So she'd moved on to other interests.

"Thank you."

"Very good, as a matter of fact."

A come-on? Certainly an effective one. Who didn't like compliments and, by extension, the people who gave them? But he sounded sincere, too. Genuinely sincere. Which made him all the more dangerous.

She went to the closet in the entryway. It was February. Daytime temperatures had been almost springlike the past few days, but nights still got cold. Trey relieved her of the cashmere coat she took out and held it open for her. His hands didn't linger on her collar, as she thought they might. She wasn't sure if she was relieved or disappointed.

Riding down in the elevator, she thanked him for picking her up, admitting she had no idea where his parents lived.

"My pleasure." He led her outside to where his car was parked. A silver Jag. It suited him. He held the door for her.

"I don't know if you remember, but we met years ago," he said as they passed through the security checkpoint of her gated community.

"Actually, I do. You've changed, though. The image that came to mind when your mother mentioned you on the phone yesterday was of a gawky adolescent, several inches shorter than you are now, thin as a rail and fighting a losing battle with zits."

He snickered good-heartedly. "That describes just about any fourteen-year-old boy. You forgot one thing, though. The hormones. As I recall, I spent most of our time together gaping at your breasts."

She laughed. "That just makes you *Everyboy.*"

He looked over, not at her chest but at her face, and smiled. "Too bad I couldn't focus my attention above your cleavage long enough to make eye contact. Who knows, I might even have said something coherent enough to suggest I was endowed with a reasonable amount of post-pubescent intelligence."

She laughed. *You're doing just fine right now.*

The corner of his mouth tilted up. "I guess it's a little late to apologize, huh?"

"Apologies are never too late, but none is required. Thanks for offering, though. If it's any consolation, I did notice more about you than the pimples."

Like the big hands and feet. The green eyes. He still had big hands. Strong hands. She glanced down at his polished brown shoes and was considering the alleged significance of a man's foot size when she decided she'd do better to fix her attention on other things.

The jade eyes. How could she have forgotten those green eyes? They were mesmerizing.

"Your mother said you live in Greensboro, too," she said.

"My condo isn't too far from yours. I used to have a place in Raleigh, but I decided a few years ago that I needed to establish some distance from the folks. Dad was cool, but Mom… She had this habit of just happening to be in the neighborhood, even though I lived clear across town, and dropping by at the most inopportune times." He glanced over. "You don't really think this dinner invitation is about making sure we're properly nourished, do you?"

She whistled a few bars of "Matchmaker."

He grinned, and she had to admit it was a very nice grin. "Exactly."

"So you're single," she remarked after a brief pause. "Ever been married?"

"Nope." He turned onto the ramp to Interstate 40. "Gabby, do you mind if I ask you a personal question?"

"Ask it and let's find out."

"Are you husband shopping?"

She gaped for a moment, then burst out laughing. "You're safe, Trey. Relax."

He heaved a dramatic sigh of relief and let his grin spread. Lordy, if only she were in predatory mode. This guy would be high on her shopping list. Very high. A real hottie…for personality, as well as looks. Easygoing self-confidence in a man was always a turn-on. Then there was his earthy frankness and sense of humor.

"So who's going to be at this dinner party?" she asked.

"Mom didn't say, but I can guess. Happily married couples with scads of perfect children. Mother isn't very subtle, but she is well-organized and a firm believer in stacking the deck, not to mention presenting good role models to emulate."

"Barbie and Ken, huh?"

"Minus the side affair with Skipper, of course."

"Two point three children, with perfect, straight teeth."

"And high honor roll report cards from the academy."

She looked over and smiled. "No zits."

"Absolutely not. They have a dermatologist on speed dial."

She laughed. "So this isn't a new experience."

"Gabby, my mother has set me up more times than I can count. And knowing your mother, she's in on tonight's conspiracy, as well."

"You seem to know my mother pretty well."

"No disrespect intended," he said.

"None taken. So where have you met her?"

He gave a halfhearted shrug. "We're on the boards of the symphony, opera and ballet. Our meetings are open to the public, by the way. You ought to attend sometime.

They'll give you a new appreciation for the nerve-racking excitement of changing spark plugs."

She chuckled. "I'll pass."

They cruised along the interstate a few miles above the speed limit, but so did most of the traffic around them. She'd learned a lot from watching people drive. Her mother, for example, was so cautious she was dangerous, one of those drivers who never got into accidents but who probably left a few in her rearview mirror. Thank God she now had a personal driver. Trey David struck her as competently aggressive, but not reckless. Another chalk mark in his favor.

"So how have you managed to escape the blissful bonds of matrimony?" she asked.

"Oh, I definitely like women, if that's what you're wondering." He glanced over and gave her a look that confirmed it. "Especially beautiful women." He veered around an articulated rig. "Actually, I am involved with someone. But she's not ready to meet my folks yet."

Gabby waited, intrigued. She was about to prompt a further explanation when he asked, "How about you? Is there a significant other in your life?"

Vaughn Steiner, she almost said. But Trey was referring to a romantic interest. No, there was no man in her life. Hadn't been for a long time. For one thing, her NASCAR schedule made an intimate friendship outside the racing circle difficult, and within it, unless they were both on the same team, a relationship brought its own complications. Mainly, though, she just hadn't met the right guy, hadn't found that perfect man who could capture her interest and imagination sufficiently to drown out all else.

She certainly wasn't attracted to the likes of Brett Conroe. Vaughn Steiner came to mind—too often, it seemed to her—but he was her team owner and out of reach. Besides, he wasn't interested in her, except as a driver.

"No," she answered simply.

A minute slipped by in silence.

"Look," Trey finally said, "can I make a suggestion?"

"Shoot."

They'd reached the outskirts of Raleigh. He exited the interstate and took a secondary road that looped around the capital city. "I've found the best way to get through these shindigs is to play along."

She studied his profile. Good enough to be minted. "Play along?"

"Pretend. I don't mean we have to hold hands or make kissy-kissy, just show a certain amount of interest in each other. Since this is our first meeting, that'll be enough for them to leave us alone and give us space.

No holding hands or kissing. Darn, she thought. That wouldn't have been a hardship, but, of course, he was right. She hadn't been lying when she said she wasn't interested in finding a husband. Too bad. Trey David seemed like a genuinely nice guy. Except that he was already spoken for. Lucky girl.

"You mean, scam our mothers?" she asked, appalled.

"Well—" he wrinkled his nose "—scam makes it sound so…undignified. I'm thinking more along the lines of misdirection and having some fun while getting them off our backs at the same time."

A slow smile curved Gabby's lips, the rebellious teenager within her roused. "Make them think their nefarious plans have worked, huh?"

He nodded. "A match made over roast beef and Yorkshire pudding.

"Skip dessert and get right to the grandkids?"

Trey laughed. "Whoa, you do move fast, Miss Race Car Driver. I don't know that I want to take it quite that far, but yeah, you get the picture."

"Okay, a reasonable approach," she admitted, "and it sounds like fun. I'm willing to play nice, but I think it's time for me to ask you a personal question. If these arranged encounters are so distasteful that you moved out of town to avoid them, why did you accept the invitation for tonight?"

He laughed and that spark of humor returned. "Oh, that's easy, Gabby. Because I wanted to see you again."

CHAPTER SIX

"VAUGHN, where are you?"

"Down here, Grace."

His mother-in-law trekked down the steps to what they called the den, the bottom-most level of the three-story house. The back wall was set into the side of the hill; the opposing wall was floor-to-ceiling glass so that the room felt as if it were part of the heavily wooded hollow over which it was suspended. Directly in view, a stream scampered among gray rocks. Most of the trees were still bare this early in the year, but that didn't detract from the majesty of the setting. Here the four seasons were always on display.

He'd been viewing a tape of yesterday's race again, this time with the sound turned off. When Grace reached the bottom step he froze the picture on the screen. Gabby was just starting to spin out.

This was his space, his sanctuary. Grace rarely came down here, except to clean, and she didn't even have to do that. He had a cleaning lady who came in three times a week to do the routine chores, dusting, vacuuming, laundry and ironing. But Grace Wilcox, who'd never had the luxury of servants, insisted the woman wasn't thorough enough and personally followed up with lemon oil and polishing cloth. Vaughn had suggested she supervise the hired help more closely if the job wasn't getting properly done, but after awhile he realized housework constituted a comfort zone for her. There was no question that the place was more immaculate and orderly than it had ever been before.

"Is everything all right?" he asked.

She glanced at the plasma screen. "If you have a few minutes, I thought we might talk."

"Of course." He switched off the system altogether and got up. Walking over to a pair of easy chairs facing the forest view, he motioned her to one while he took the other. "What's up?"

She perched on the edge of the seat, her back straight, and he knew whatever she had to say was serious enough to make her uncomfortable.

"I've been meaning to talk to you about this for some time, but…well, I haven't been sure how to approach it."

Please, God, he prayed, *don't let her tell me she wants to move out.*

Grace had come to live with him and Stephanie right after Lisa died, and he would be eternally grateful for her support. He and his mother-in-law had gotten along well enough before Lisa's accident, but after she died he'd become dependent on Grace to take care of Stephanie, to give their lives some semblance of family and normalcy.

A grandma isn't the same as a mom, but Grace had done everything she could to help the girl cope. It couldn't have been easy for the widow who'd raised her only child single-handed, only to lose her in a senseless accident. If Grace blamed Vaughn for Lisa's death, she never voiced it. If she resented his survival, she never showed it. She'd soldiered on without complaint and dedicated herself to raising her granddaughter. Maybe not with as much cozy warmth as some grandmothers might, but certainly with the kind of levelheaded steadfastness that helped give the six-year-old a taproot of stability.

"I'm worried about Stephanie," she said.

At this angle he caught a glimpse of Lisa, saw how she might have looked in twenty years. Had she lived.

The flash jolted him and added to his sense of loss. Sometimes he wished he'd been the one to die that night—survivor's guilt, a counselor had called it—then he wouldn't have to go on without a mate, with a ruined arm, with a ruined career. And he wouldn't have to see the desolation in his daughter's eyes. But he had survived, and Stephanie was the reason he went on.

"Is she sick?"

"Not physically." Grace looked down and smoothed out the folds of her calf-length, embroidered-denim skirt. "But she misses her mother so much."

"We all do."

The psychologist had said his young daughter might recover from the tragedy quickly with only occasional relapses, or the active grieving process could linger for a long time. He thought after two years—a long time for a six-year-old—Stephanie had reached the acceptance stage, but apparently he'd been mistaken.

Grace stilled her hands and folded them in her lap. "I try to do what I think Lisa would want—"

"Grace, I can't tell you how much your being here means to Steph. And to me. I don't know how either of us could have managed without you."

"But that's the thing," she said, looking up. "Stephanie misses you, too."

"Misses me? I'm still here."

But not a lot. Building two new NASCAR teams from the ground up wasn't a nine-to-five job. Over the last two years there had been endless meetings with sponsors and potential sponsors, almost always on their turf, which meant nearly constant traveling. Ditto for conferences with public relations managers, suppliers for everything from decals to souvenir items to private jets. Then strategy and tactics sessions with crew chiefs and drivers, plus the time at the track itself before, during and after races, not to mention the hours spent with accountants who documented every penny of the tens of millions of dollars a NASCAR team went through. The all-consuming nature of the racing business was an occupational hazard. He hadn't had much more time available for his family when he'd been a driver, because then he'd also had to do product endorsements for sponsors. But Stephanie'd had a mother back then, a mother who'd gloried in her role as a mom and was good at it, a woman who'd been a loving wife…

"She's not worried about my safety, is she? Stephanie knows I'm not driving anymore."

He'd been involved in half a dozen crashes since she was born, wrecks big enough to destroy the cars he'd been driving, and he'd walked away from all of them with nothing more than a few scratches. Serious injuries were rare, even in the worst-looking pileups. All that, however, had been before Lisa had disappeared from Stephanie's life. Besides, at her age, she wouldn't remember much, if anything, about those incidents. Under the present circumstances, though, regardless of the nature of his occupation, it would be perfectly normal for her to worry about losing her father whenever he wasn't around.

"It's just that you're not here very much," Grace said, confirming what he already knew. "Steph gets to see you maybe one or two days a week for a few hours. Then you're gone, and she's terrified that you're not coming back."

He rubbed his face with both hands. He hadn't realized. Maybe staying in racing had been a mistake. Maybe he should have done something else—or nothing at all. He wasn't destitute. He'd earned a lot of money driving over the years, and even though they'd lived well and spent liberally, they'd saved, too. But not work? And if not racing, then what? How would he continue to be who he was if he couldn't be around the noise, the smell, the vibrations of race cars?

Stephanie always greeted him with smiles and affection when they were together. That was probably why he'd had no idea she was still so scared, so worried about losing him. He thought she understood why he had to be away as much as he was, but he realized now he was putting an awful lot of pressure on a six-year-old girl whose life had been turned upside down.

"You think I'm neglecting her?"

He'd do anything for his little girl, even give up the only occupation he knew, if he had to. His whole life had revolved around auto racing, from the time he was Stephanie's age, even younger.

At five, he'd "borrowed" a neighbor's soap box, pointed it down a hill and damn near killed himself. After suitable counseling, his father had taken him to an amusement park, put a helmet on his head and bought him rides in go-carts.

A year later he'd gotten his first quarter midget. He wasn't satisfied with the way it performed, so he started tinkering with the little two-cycle engine. His father came home from work one day, saw parts scattered all over one of his mother's new sheets on the garage floor and ordered him to put it all back together again. Vaughn did, with no pieces left over. It didn't run any better than it had before, but it didn't run any worse, either. The sheet didn't fare nearly as well. It took him a month to earn enough money doing extra chores to pay for it. That inside peek into the mysterious workings of an internal combustion engine, however, had opened a whole new world to him. The cost of a sheet had been worth it.

After that came a midget car and more tinkering. He was racing at a local dirt track long before he had a driver's license—on private property and under his dad's supervision. His mother complained about the grease on his clothes, but she bragged to her friends and neighbors that she always knew where to find him.

He'd pored over every book and magazine about cars he could find, studied the mechanics of engines, learned about the people who raced them. Nobody challenged him on statistics. He could rattle off numbers, down to decimal points of horsepower. He knew who won what when, in what cars and the speeds they'd clocked. He bored people stiff with his arcane knowledge, except those who shared his obsession.

By the time he entered high school he was racing dragsters, and winning. By then he could also tear down a supercharged V-8, reassemble it in record time and leave it running smoother, faster and more efficiently than it had before.

From there he advanced to stock cars and the real fun began. Everything up to that point, he soon realized, had been preparation and education. He'd found his real home.

When he was seventeen he won his first stock car race and met Lisa, who'd shown up with a guy by the name of

Jem Nordstrom, at a dirt track outside Charlotte. Vaughn won by a full car length. After that, there was no turning back—from racing or Lisa.

His father had lived long enough to see him win his first NASCAR Busch race before cancer killed him. His mother had witnessed his first NASCAR NEXTEL Cup before a burst aneurysm took her, as well.

Then, a year later, Lisa was gone.

"Not neglecting, Vaughn," Grace said now, shaking him out of his reverie. She reached over and rested a hand on his, an uncharacteristically sympathetic and affectionate gesture for her. She had never been the touchy-feely type, even with Lisa. "I know you love Stephanie and so does she. But if you could find some way to spend more time with her, I think it would help a lot."

"Has she been acting up? Complaining?"

"Not complaining. I'm not sure she's fully aware of what's bothering her, but she has been acting up in school lately."

"In what way? I thought she loved school."

Grace bit her bottom lip. "Getting into fights with the other kids, talking back to the teacher."

Vaughn was about to say Grace should have told him, but, of course, that was exactly what she was doing now. It all added to his sense of failure. He'd failed Lisa when she'd needed him most, and now he was failing his daughter. What kind of man was he, anyway?

"Do you think she needs more counseling?" he asked.

After Lisa's death Vaughn had arranged for the three of them to receive grief counseling together. At least initially. After a few weeks his attention had been diverted when his doctor had informed him that the damage to his arm was probably permanent, that he would never regain its full use and strength. That his NASCAR driving career was over. For him the only therapy had been work. Since he hadn't been ready to leave the world of NASCAR, it was then he had decided to start his own team.

"What Stephanie needs more than anything," Grace said forcefully to recapture his attention, "is to see and spend more time with her father."

CHAPTER SEVEN

TREY TURNED OFF THE MAIN thoroughfare and took a narrow road that wound into the hills around Raleigh. The maples and oaks were still bare, the evergreens still wearing their dark winter coats. In a month the delicate pastels of spring would wash through the woods bringing light and vibrancy.

A mile or two later he pulled up in front of a pillared estate entrance, reached over the sun visor and pressed a button. The scrolled iron gates swung slowly inward. He drove through, hit the button again and waited to insure the gates were securely closed behind them before proceeding on.

A quarter mile farther up a tree-lined drive, a two-and-a-half-story house of redbrick and white stone with four chimneys and a black-slate roof stood atop a sprawling knoll. The front door swung open before they reached it, and a middle-aged woman in a gray-and-white maid's uniform greeted "Mr. Trey." He introduced Gabby as Josephine took her coat and purse. Trey then escorted Gabby into a large living room dominated by a carved marble fireplace where a low-flame hardwood fire glowed.

Trey's mother came forward to greet her latest guest, bejeweled hands extended, palms down. Gabby had met Marjorie David on a variety of occasions over the years. Marjorie was a good ten years older than her own mother, but the two women could have been sisters. Both were large, well-padded matrons who clearly enjoyed dressing up. This evening the hostess was wearing a peach-colored satin dress that bespoke understated elegance.

"I'm delighted you could join us, Gabriella. Your mother's been telling us all about your busy schedule. It all sounds so very exciting." She backed up a step, extending her hold on Gabby's hands. "And you look absolutely lovely, my dear. Doesn't she, Trey?"

"Absolutely," he agreed, and gave Gabby a wink.

Gabby's mother, wearing a calf-length blue-silk outfit Gabby had never seen before, came up and gave her a peck on the cheek. "Aren't you glad you took my advice?" she whispered. Unspoken was "for a change." Gabby wondered if she was referring to the dress or the man standing beside her.

"Thank you so much for bringing her," Della said to Trey, as if Cinderella couldn't find her way out of her pumpkin without him.

"Oh, I can assure you it was my pleasure, Mrs. O'Farrell. She gave me some valuable tips on how to evade the cops in a car chase."

Della stared at him, then accusingly at her daughter.

"Now, dear," Marjorie said with a click of her tongue, "why ever would you want to evade the police?"

He put his arm around his mother in a gesture of pure affection. "I'm teasing, Mom. I'd be more likely to be running from my creditors," he muttered in an aside to Della. "My gambling debts get out of hand sometimes. The last time I had my legs broken it took forever for them to heal."

With a chuckle Trey's father, Reggie, came forward. A

distinguished-looking man with silver hair and a rosy complexion, he wasn't nearly as tall as his son, but he outweighed him by at least fifty pounds.

"Don't believe a word he tells you, Della." He extended his hand to Gabby. "Don't mind Trey. Poor boy. He can't help making up tall tales." He lowered his voice into a conspiratorial whisper that everyone could hear. "He gets it from his mother's side of the family, you know. Her uncle was a politician."

"Reginald David, that's a terrible thing to say," his wife huffed, but it was easy to see this was an old routine. She barged between them, and arm in arm, escorted Gabby farther into the room to make introductions while Trey fetched flutes of champagne.

Nathan Crenshaw was in his late forties and had recently taken over as head of a family owned investment company. His rather plump wife, Louise, was well-known for raising enormous sums of money for shelters for battered women and children. They had six kids, four of whom were adopted. Gabby had met Louise before and liked her. It was also clear that her husband doted on her.

The Braddocks were a few years younger, in their early forties. Short and wiry, Willard Braddock was the president of an import-export company. His wife, Janelle, slipped her hand into his. "Rooster was so pleased when I told him you would be here. He just loves NASCAR."

Della arched a brow, drew in her chin and reached for her cocktail glass, making Gabby wonder if it was at the successful executive's nickname or the reference to NASCAR that irritated her. The Braddocks, she learned a moment later, had four children, undoubtedly with perfect teeth, or at least braces to make them that way—and they, too, were NASCAR fans.

The Harpers, Mitch and Molly, were next. In their mid-thirties, they absolutely radiated youth and energy. Unlike the other men, Mitch wasn't wearing a conservative suit and tie but a rather loud sport jacket and open-necked knit shirt. Molly, whose hair was an unnaturally bright shade of red, was the only woman wearing pants. Silk, to be sure, but completely at odds with the other women's dresses. Gabby surmised they'd been told the occasion was informal and had confused the term with casual, not realizing informal meant no tuxes or evening gowns.

Insuring there wouldn't be an odd number at the table, Marjorie's younger brother, Dr. Norman Esau, a medical missionary home on his biannual sabbatical from Africa, had joined them.

Trey and Gabby were seated midtable next to each other, directly across from the Harpers, who, it turned out, owned Vitality Health Clubs, which were now expanding nation-wide. They also had three children, the youngest of whom was barely two years old—but already showing signs of being a prodigy, Gabby was sure.

"I watched the California race on Sunday," Molly said. "I was so disappointed when you didn't get to finish. It must have been terrifying, doing wheelies with all those cars coming at you at two hundred miles an hour."

Gabby brushed it aside. "Actually, I was only doing about a hundred and eighty."

"Still," Molly persisted. "I'd be scared to death."

"It's really not as dangerous as it looks," Rooster said. "The way the cars are designed, the driver sits in a kind of steel cage, like a capsule. The seat itself is very snug, the five-point harness ensures the driver won't be thrown around and the helmets are custom fitted." All of a sudden he seemed to realize he wasn't the expert at the table. "Isn't that right?" he asked Gabby.

"Completely. We're very well protected," she agreed. "That's why cars can roll and flip half a dozen times and the driver still climbs out and walks away."

"Good heavens," Marjorie exclaimed, and looked at Della.

"Did you always know you wanted to drive race cars?" Mitch asked.

Gabby shook her head. "Actually, I came to it very late. Most NASCAR drivers know from childhood that they want to race. I didn't even see my first NASCAR event until my senior year in college. Billy Beau, my date—

"His real name is William Beauregard Hazelworth," Della interjected. "Of the Baltimore Hazelworths. Family goes back to colonial times. Such a nice young man. I don't know why you ever stopped seeing him."

Gabby clicked her tongue. "Because he went into the seminary and became a Trappist monk, Mother."

"Well," Della huffed undeterred, "maybe if you had been more encouraging..."

Trey snickered, provoking a scowl from his mother.

"Anyway," Gabby went on, "Billy invited me to a NASCAR race at Dover. I'd never given much thought to stock car racing, but Billy assured me I'd enjoy it. Turned out he was absolutely right. The noise, the speed, the excitement. Billy had gotten passes to the pit area, and I was editor of the school newspaper at the time, so after the race I wrangled an interview with the winning driver."

"And that was?" Molly drawled, her dark brows raised in anticipation.

"Vaughn Steiner."

"The man who owns your team now," Braddock said.

Gabby nodded. "He was friendly, easygoing—"

"And easy to look at, huh?" Janelle interjected.

Incredibly easy. A good face. With character. Intelligence and an infectious inclination to smile.

"He answered all my naive questions without making me feel stupid, and that was all it took. One day at the races, an interview with a driver and I was totally hooked."

Trey covered her hand with his. The sensation wasn't unpleasant, but it was unexpected. Gabby instinctively started to pull her hand out from under his.

"Check out your mother," he said so close to her ear that from the far end of the table, it probably looked like he was kissing her.

Della was staring with obvious approval at their joined hands.

"Hooked, huh?" Trey asked.

"Like a fish on a worm."

"A frog on a fly."

"My mother on Prada." They heard a muted growl from the end of the table.

"A man on a beautiful woman," Trey said.

Molly went "Ooh."

Mitch muttered a delighted, "Yeah."

The Braddocks snickered, while Marjorie and Della eyed each other with not totally disapproving scowls.

"That's how you became a spectator," Trey said. "But how did you get into doing it?" His face was turned to Gabby so only she could see the wink he gave her.

Straining to control the urge to giggle, Gabby reversed her hand and they interlaced their fingers.

"Um, what did you say? Oh, when did I start doing it? That didn't happen until a year later. I'd done some modeling for a fashion designer while I was in college and stayed with it for a while after graduating, so I wasn't able to get to a whole lot of NASCAR races, but there was a drag strip not too far from where I was living. I hired one of the drivers to coach me, then I entered a race."

"She didn't tell me a thing about it, of course," Della huffed.

"Dad knew, and he didn't mind," Gabby pointed out.

"Did you win?" Mitch asked.

She let out a guffaw. "Came in dead last. Didn't matter. I wanted to do it over and over."

"Sounds a lot like sex," Trey remarked.

Everyone went silent, then Gabby and Mitch exploded with laughter. Molly choked on the sip of wine she was taking. Everyone laughed, except Della, who looked like she'd just bitten into an apple and found half a worm.

"You refused to give it up, didn't you?" Trey asked.

"Sex?"

"Gabriella," Della intoned from down the table. "Please."

"I did it every weekend I could after that."

"Couldn't get enough, huh?"

"Not on your life."

"Practice makes perfect?"

"Play your cards right and maybe you'll find out."

"Oh, my," Molly giggled, and reached for her husband's hand. He took it and smiled at the others, as if he'd just been found out.

"Racing, I mean." Gabby snickered. "Little by little I improved."

"You weren't intimidated by the speed, the competition…the hazards?" Louise asked.

"Intimidated?" Gabby asked. "Just the opposite. Danger adds to the excitement. The vibrations under my feet, the rush in the air, the agitation of the crowds…"

"It's intoxicating, isn't it?" Mitch said.

"When is your next race, my dear?" Louise asked.

"Las Vegas, in two weeks."

"Oh, how exciting," Molly exclaimed. "I just love Vegas."

"Sin City," Trey remarked, tightening his hold on Gabby's hand. "Quickie marriages."

Gabby cozied up to him, her eyes pools of girlish adoration. "Who needs society weddings in a big church when you can get the deed done in a wedding chapel by an Elvis impersonator?"

Marjorie went as pale as the tablecloth, and Della's butter knife clattered onto her bread plate, her mouth open.

Tsk, tsk. Very unladylike, Gabby thought with amusement.

Nathan Crenshaw, sitting beside Della, patted her on the shoulder. Meanwhile, Reggie peered intently at his son from the head of the table and subtly shook his head in reprimand, but there was no mistaking the trace of a smile on his lips.

After things settled down a minute later, Molly asked, "What's Vaughn Steiner like?"

"I was sure he was going to win his third NASCAR NEXTEL Cup," her husband said, "till that unfortunate accident."

CHAPTER EIGHT

"A RACING ACCIDENT?" asked Janelle Braddock.

"No, no," Gabby was quick to reply. "A couple of years ago he and his wife were spending a weekend at a friend's horse farm up in Virginia. They went for a moonlight ride after dinner and Lisa's horse bolted. It might have been spooked by a snake, but nobody knows for sure. Lisa was caught off guard and slipped off the saddle, but her foot got hung up in the stirrup and she was dragged. She died of head injuries a few hours later."

"Oh, my God," several people said simultaneously. "How terrible."

"Vaughn galloped after her and grabbed the rein. In trying to save her, his right arm was wrenched so violently that he dislocated his shoulder. They reset it of course, but he suffered some sort of nerve damage. He's lost some strength and dexterity in the arm, enough that it ended his driving career."

"Probably Reflex Sympathetic Dystrophy Syndrome," Dr. Esau contributed. He'd been quiet up until then, seemingly content to observe and listen. "It can be quite debilitating. Symptoms range from mild discomfort to chronic burning sensations."

"Is there a cure?" Molly asked.

He shook his head. "Analgesics, including narcotics, can alleviate some of the pain, but they're only palliative. Medication can't correct the underlying nerve damage, which might be permanent."

Gabby wished she could go back to bantering with Trey and driving her mother crazy. She didn't want to think about what Vaughn had gone through, what he was still having to endure everyday. She'd seen the hunger in his eyes when he thought no one was looking. The mournful stare, the melancholy breaths, the way he flexed his right hand as cars circled the track during practice sessions. He'd lost the woman he loved and the career that had been the focus of his life. She wondered what it would be like to be loved by a man who committed himself so fully.

AFTER DINNER the party adjourned to the living room for coffee and dessert. Trying to recapture the earlier light mood, Gabby led Trey by the hand to one of the love seats in front of the fireplace. They sat thigh to thigh, fingers entwined.

Della, no doubt determined to steer the conversation away from her daughter's unsuitable current career and the tragedies suffered by her team owner, started to expound on her previous accomplishments, but Gabby would have none of it. She asked the other guests about their families, businesses and ambitions. People were usually eager to talk about themselves, especially if it gave them an opportunity to brag.

"Where did you go to college?" Mitch asked Trey. The bodybuilder had earlier admitted he hadn't finished at State because he didn't have the money. Now, with a growing family and thriving business, he didn't have the time. Maybe someday, he said.

"Duke," Trey answered simply.

"He majored in business and marketing," his mother added. "Graduated at the top of his class."

"Did you go to work for your dad's company right away?" Molly asked.

"I started off there," Trey admitted, "but left after a few months?"

"Why? Sounds like a perfect setup."

"Except that nobody was willing to tell me, the boss's son, when I was wrong or that there might be a better way to do things." Trey folded his free hand over Gabby's and smiled coyly at her. "We don't learn from our successes but from our mistakes."

"But you're working there now," Janelle commented, more statement than question.

"He just took over as vice president for public relations and promotions," Marjorie said.

Della eyed Gabby to see if she was paying attention.

"Oneida Gilbert handled our advertising program for years," Reggie said, "and did a wonderful job, but when she decided to retire, I used the opportunity to create the VP position and asked Trey to come back."

"The challenge you'd been waiting for?" Rooster asked.

"What is life without challenges?" Trey responded, and again met Gabby's eyes. She hoped the people around them didn't realize the smile they exchanged was actually the suppression of an impulse to burst out laughing.

"We really should be going, Trey," she said a few minutes later in a tone that could have been construed as intimate.

"Yes, we should." He rose, still holding her hand, and helped her to her feet.

Even more softly so that no one could hear her, she

whispered, "Get me out of here before I crack up and ruin everything."

"Yes, dear," he murmured, which didn't help.

After the mandatory good-nights, Trey escorted her to his car. It had turned decidedly cold since their arrival and the light breeze that had come up added to the frosty chill. She shivered in her coat, which was all the invitation he needed to put his arm around her.

At the passenger door to the Jaguar he inclined his head to her. "We're being observed."

She gazed up at him with baby-blue eyes. "Let's give them something to talk about."

She raised her arms and linked her fingers behind his neck. Smiling, she said, "It's been a fun evening, Trey."

"Thanks for being such a good sport." He kissed her on the cheek.

"It's not over, darling."

He brought his mouth down to hers.

She was tempted to tell him they could do better but backed off. She didn't want to start a fire that might blaze out of control.

He dragged out the process of settling her in the passenger seat, even slipped on her seat belt for her, then he ran like a fugitive around the vehicle and climbed behind the wheel.

"So what's going on between you and Steiner?" Trey asked as he pulled out of the driveway.

CHAPTER NINE

VAUGHN THOUGHT HARD about Grace's comments as he was getting ready for bed later that night. She was right, of course. He needed to spend more time with his daughter. The problem wasn't will or desire but that precious commodity itself. Somehow he would have to make more of it available, quality time.

Unfortunately he had to leave tomorrow for a conference in Chicago with one of his sponsors, then on to Denver and Dallas for more meetings. He wouldn't see his daughter again until Wednesday afternoon.

As he lay in bed he was reminded once more of how much he missed Lisa, missed her resourcefulness, her smile and, yes, her body. He was determined not to keep reliving that horrible night, but he had learned that it was impossible to order his mind not to think about a subject.

That long weekend had started out so perfectly. They were staying at the guesthouse on Bud Dresden's horse farm, where they had all the privacy they could possibly ask for, privacy that had become a luxury since his rise in the NASCAR world.

Everything had been going so right for them. Professionally he'd been doing well on the track and had a good chance of winning the NASCAR NEXTEL Cup Championship for the third time in a row. No one had ever done that, which meant he would be making history. Even if someone matched his record later, he would forever be the first NASCAR driver to win three years in a row. Personally his marriage was everything the story books promised, the union of two people in harmony with each other. And they had an adorable daughter who was smart and happy.

Those three days away were supposed to be a reward for both of them, a chance to be alone, to reconnect, to lounge and make leisurely love. And they had. Everything had been perfect until that moonlight ride.

In less than five minutes the world changed completely.

Lisa was dead.

He was injured in a way that not only robbed him of a record-making year, but of a career, the only career he'd ever wanted.

Worst of all, his bright, precocious four-year-old daughter was left motherless.

He lay on his back and waited for the pill he'd taken to kick in, for the searing pain that was now a permanent part of his life to subside enough for him to sleep. While he waited, he massaged his right forearm. The weakness was frustrating. He could still write; he could still grasp light objects. But he couldn't dunk a basketball or turn a wrench. He could drive, but he couldn't slam a gear lever with the speed and precision that years of professional racing had honed to an instinctive reflex.

He had to concentrate now on what he could do, not what he couldn't. But people like Jem Nordstrom didn't make that easy.

Jem was wrong about a couple of things, though.

For example, Gabby O'Farrell was no girl. She was a

woman. And she was no Sunday driver. She was a race car driver with extraordinary skill and plenty of untapped potential.

Yeah, she'd screwed up in California, but, Vaughn realized, so had he. He knew Jem had a tendency to ease off early on curves. Why hadn't he warned her?

The answer was that until he'd said it to Gabby, he hadn't given it conscious thought. It was something he'd picked up and integrated into an automatic response. The trouble was that Gabby hadn't had the same depth of experience with Jem, so how was she supposed to know?

As he tossed in his bed, Vaughn also remembered the episode with Brett Conroe and his parting shot.

You have the hots for her.

Ridiculous.

Okay, so he looked at her. Of course he did. Gabby O'Farrell was a beautiful woman, and injured or not, Vaughn was still a man, a man who hadn't been with a woman since Lisa. For a long time after she died he wasn't interested in female companionship. In his own mind he was still married. He'd never wandered from his vows when Lisa was alive, never even been tempted. She'd been all he needed, all he wanted, everything he had ever hoped for. He still loved her. He always would. But...

She was gone from his life, physically at least.

Of course he looked at Gabby, he ruminated as he turned over, trying to find a comfortable position. How could any man not look at her? The soft brown hair, the tantalizing blue eyes that were so expressive they made it impossible for her to hide her deepest emotions. Like when she looked at him yesterday after the race, begging him to go easy on her.

You have the hots for her.

He needed a woman in his life, but not Gabby O'Farrell. Not a spoiled society debutante.

He'd studied the driving records of dozens of drivers in the NASCAR NEXTEL Cup Series and the NASCAR Busch Series before inviting Gabby and Brett to join his team.

Brett had been an easy choice. Young, good behind the wheel, with an excellent record in the NASCAR Busch Series, he also had the looks and personal charisma that would win him a faithful fan following as well as sponsor support. Being a bachelor didn't hurt his appeal with female fans, either. Most important, though, was that he had racing in his blood.

Gabby was a different story. It wasn't her relative lack of experience that had made him hesitate to take her on. It wasn't her being a woman, though he had to admit it, too, had given him pause.

He'd compared her record with the men he was considering. She'd scored high, among the top half dozen, so he went to see Clyde Remundo, her car owner in the NASCAR Busch Series.

"Heard you were shopping around," Clyde said, his trademark toothpick stuck in the corner of his mouth. "Wondered how long it would take for you to get around to her."

"She that good?"

"I reckon you've checked her record."

"Statistics can be deceiving."

Clyde chuckled. "You got that right, but it's those numbers that determine whether you're a winner or a loser."

"In which of those two categories does Gabby O'Farrell fit?"

Clyde shifted the toothpick to the other side of his mouth. "She's good, has the potential to be a big winner."

"So you don't want to let her go," Vaughn stated, not surprised.

"Hell, no. But I will if this is the right move for her."

"Why wouldn't it be?"

Clyde shrugged. "Not everyone's cut out to be a NEXTEL level competitor."

"You don't think she has what it takes to hold up under the strain?"

The NASCAR Busch Series was highly competitive but the pressures off the track weren't nearly as intense as those on NASCAR NEXTEL drivers, where the money was considerably greater and the demands for earning it were even higher.

"She's got what it takes," Clyde stated.

"But?" Vaughn asked. "You have reservations?"

Clyde considered a minute, flicked away his toothpick, got a fresh one out of his shirt pocket and stuck it between his teeth.

"How much do you know about her background?"

"I know she's the daughter of Brock O'Farrell, that her mother is Philadelphia mainline, society's upper crust, that Gabby herself graduated from Bryn Mawr in the top ten percent of her class, and that in the four years she's been in the Busch Series she's accumulated an impressive record."

"Statistics," Clyde muttered.

"So what don't they tell me?"

"Gabby O'Farrell is probably one of the best drivers I've seen in the last ten, fifteen years. And she's all gung-ho about racing. Today. Tomorrow she's liable to wake up and decide she wants to become a chef and open a restaurant or marry a celebrity and have a slew of kids or become a movie star. She sure has the assets," he added with a wink.

"I think she'd be damn good on your team, Vaughn. Just be prepared in case she decides in the middle of the season she doesn't want to do it anymore."

Clyde dug his fists into the pockets of his overalls. "Heard you been talking to Brett Conroe about joining you."

Vaughn hadn't advertised the fact, but he wasn't surprised Clyde knew about it. NASCAR was a small community. There was jealous respect for privacy, but there weren't many secrets.

"Yeah," Vaughn acknowledged.

"There's your stability then. My gut tells me he's not as good as Gabby *could* be, but I don't think he'll let you down."

In the end there was one other deciding factor that weighed very heavily in Vaughn's decision to ask Gabby to join his team.

She came complete with a sponsor: O'Farrell Industries. It was hard to turn down a ten-million-dollar sponsorship package.

CHAPTER TEN

DELLA O'FARRELL lived in Raleigh where the corporate offices of O'Farrell Industries were headquartered, but on the Friday evening following the dinner party at the Davids she decided to drive to Greensboro to have an impromptu dinner with her daughter.

Gabby was surprised to see her. She was also annoyed. She had to leave early the next morning for a series of guest appearances on her way to Las Vegas and was hoping for a quiet evening at home, maybe her last free Friday until the end of the racing season.

She couldn't help but laugh, too. She knew what she was in for, a long list of questions about Trey. Had they seen each other since Monday night? No. Wasn't he handsome? Yes. And charming? Yes again. Do you like him? Yes. Are you going to see him again? Maybe.

"It's good of you to drive all the way down here just to see me." Gabby turned off Guilford College Road and headed for the Japanese hibachi steak house her mother had agreed to, a sign of her desperation to share her daughter's company, since Della wasn't much of a steak eater. The restaurant also served seafood, however, which Della loved, so it wasn't as if Gabby was intent on making her mother suffer.

Since it was only a little past six, early for most diners, the place wasn't yet crowded and they were immediately escorted to a large steel grill. Two other couples were already seated there, leaving two more places open.

Gabby and her mother were offered drinks. Because she was driving, Gabby opted for iced tea. Della requested a glass of Chardonnay.

The drinks had just arrived when Gabby looked up to see Vaughn standing at the hostess's station. Beside him was a blond-haired girl of about six. His daughter most likely, for she had his features, but not his eyes. Hers were a soft blue.

His sweeping survey of the room stopped when he saw Gabby, and her pulse instantly ratcheted up a few beats. She pointed to the two empty seats beside her and motioned for him to join her and her mother.

"Mom," she said when they came over, "you remember Vaughn Steiner, my team owner."

Della extended her hand. "How very nice to see you again, Mr. Steiner."

They had met several months earlier at the public relations extravaganza set up to announce OI's sponsorship of Gabby in the NASCAR NEXTEL Cup Series. The process had been initiated by Gabby's father and the final details worked out by OI's contracting department and lawyers. Privately it had been rumored that Della wasn't enthusiastic about the deal, but pulling out of it after her husband's death would have stirred up a hornet's nest with Gabby and started Della off on the wrong foot with the board of directors that had already approved the expenditure, not to mention the negative publicity that could have ensued. So she'd played her role with her accustomed dignity and charm.

"This is my daughter, Stephanie," Vaughn said, proudly

placing his left hand on her shoulder. "Steph, this is Mrs. O'Farrell."

The girl had hardly finished her polite greeting of the older woman when she turned to Gabby.

"I saw you at Daytona. You were awesome."

Gabby couldn't help but smile. "Thank you. I wish I could have done as well—" she gave Vaughn a quick glance "—in California."

"That wasn't your fault. Jem Nordstrom's a jerk. I heard Daddy say so."

Catching the mildly embarrassed grin on Vaughn's face, Gabby laughed. "Well, I think we can all agree on that. Please join us."

A woman at the other end of the table spoke up. "You're Vaughn Steiner, aren't you?" She looked at Gabby, as if trying to decide. "And you're Gabby O'Farrell. I thought I recognized you, but I wasn't sure. You're not as famous as Vaughn, but I bet someday you will be."

"What a nice thing to say," Gabby replied.

"I can't believe I'm sitting at the same table with Vaughn Steiner and Gabby O'Farrell. Dave," she said, giving the man beside her a poke in the ribs, "I told you we should have brought the camera. Nobody'll believe it when I tell them. Two of the most famous people in NASCAR and we're having dinner with them!"

"Maisey, why don't you leave them in peace to enjoy their meal?"

"But, Dave, the food hasn't even arrived yet."

The man addressed Vaughn. "My wife sometimes forgets her manners when she gets excited."

"I'm complimented," Vaughn said with a smile. "Just don't blab if I spill rice all over my lap."

Maisey poked her husband again. "See, I told you he was nice."

The waitress arrived and took their orders. Steak and shrimp for everyone, except Della who requested scallops and shrimp.

The other couple joined the conversation after their orders were in, and the focus shifted to Gabby, since she was currently the only woman driver in the NASCAR NEXTEL Cup Series.

Finally the chef came to the table and put on his demonstration with knife and fork, slicing the tails off the shrimp in quick, flamboyant but precise movements. He flipped one of the tails into the air and caught it in the high crown of his chef's hat. Another he tossed over his shoulder into a bowl he held behind his back. Stephanie watched with rapt attention.

The chef finished grilling the food and began distributing generous portions. Soon the other couples at the table had reverted to quiet conversation among themselves.

"Do you come here often?" Gabby asked the girl.

"This is the first time. Daddy has to go away again tomorrow. I won't see him until next week. Do you work on cars, too? Daddy used to until he hurt his arm. Mommy always made him wash his hands in the garage before he came into the house, so he wouldn't get grease all over everything."

"I'm not much of a mechanic," Gabby said. "Actually, I'm not a mechanic at all. I know basically how engines work, but I leave making them go fast to experts. How about you? Do you like working on cars and engines?"

"Daddy used to let me hold the tools for him and give him the right ones, but we don't do that anymore, 'cause of his hand."

The sadness in the girl's words was unmistakable.

"It must be difficult being away so much," Della said to Vaughn. "Don't you get tired of all the travel?"

"I've been doing it so long, Mrs. O'Farrell, I think I'd go stir-crazy if I didn't. I just wish I could spend more time with Steph, but I have to go where the races are."

"Who takes care of her while you're away? Do you have a live-in nanny?"

"Better than that. Steph's grandmother, my mother-in-law, lives with us."

Gabby turned to Stephanie. "Is your grandmother a NASCAR fan, too?"

The child raised her shoulders and lowered them. "I guess. She watches the races with me but..."

Gabby leaned toward her. "I keep having to explain the rules to my mom. I bet you have the same problem with your grandmother."

The girl's face broke into a smile. "Yeah," she whispered. "Seems like she's always asking the same questions, too." After another mouthful of food, she added, "I told her about you being the only girl driver."

"And what did she say?"

"That she couldn't understand why a grown woman would want to drive that fast."

"I've often asked the same question," Della contributed.

"Did you tell her for the same reason men do?" Gabby asked. "Going fast is fun. It has nothing to do about being a boy or a girl."

"Grandma says it's all right for boys, 'cause they're different, but girls should know better."

"Your grandmother sounds like a very wise woman," Della put in.

"But I want to race cars, too," Stephanie objected. "Just like Gabby."

"What does your dad say?" Gabby asked, giving him a quick eye.

Stephanie looked up at him, and Gabby saw love in her gaze and something else. Worry? Sadness? Loneliness? "He says I can do anything I want to."

"You know, that's what my dad told me, too, and he was a very smart man."

Vaughn looked over at her and raised an eyebrow, a smile of amusement and appreciation curling the corners of his mouth.

He was eating with his left hand. She'd seen him do it before, though she knew he was naturally right-handed. Her mother was watching him, as well, as though she really was expecting him to drop his food.

OVER THE COURSE of the meal Vaughn made several valiant attempts to engage Della in conversation, asking her the usual questions about where she was originally from. Philadelphia. If she still had family there? Yes. Did she get to see them very much? No. It became quickly apparent she wasn't interested in talking, at least not to him. He wondered if he had done or said something to offend her. He couldn't imagine what. They'd only met once and that occasion had been very friendly, if impersonal. Perhaps joining her and Gabby had interrupted a mother-daughter conversation.

He contented himself with listening to the happy chatter between Gabby and his daughter. And it was happy. The sparkle in the child's eyes had been reignited, and it made Vaughn that much more aware of how much his daughter had changed since Lisa's death.

He had been uncomfortable when he spied Gabby here in the restaurant. Pleased and annoyed at the same time. He'd brought Stephanie here without Grace, so they could spend the evening together. He hadn't planned on sharing Steph with strangers, but listening to her bubbly conversation with Gabby, he was glad they'd run into each other.

"Oh, I can't believe it. Oh, my God. Look, June. It's Vaughn Steiner and Gabby O'Farrell."

They both looked up to see two women standing a few feet away, their faces lit up in wonder.

"Oh, my God. You're right. It is them." The second woman put her hands to her mouth, her eyes as big as salad plates.

The first one rummaged frantically in her oversized purse, dropping tissues, keys and a cell phone on the floor in her haste. A passing busgirl dutifully helped pick them up.

"Where is that thing?" The first woman grumbled in panic. "I always carry it with me. Here." She triumphantly held up a leather-bound autograph pad and stepped over to the table.

"Mr. Steiner, Ms. O'Farrell, I'm so excited to meet you both. Oh, my God, I can't believe I'm standing here talking to you." She flipped through the pages of her book and found a blank one, then thrust it forward. "Can I get your autographs, please? Wait till I tell Velma. She won't believe this."

Vaughn accepted the pad. The woman only then realizing he didn't have a pen.

"I've got one here someplace." She started rummaging again through her bag. "I always carry pens with me."

Gabby reached into her own purse, pulled out a roller gel and handed it to him.

He asked the woman's name and where she was from. The woman was ready to give him her life's story, if he'd asked for it. Vaughn slowly wrote an inscription and handed the book to Gabby. Meanwhile the second woman was mumbling that now she couldn't find her pad, she must have left it out when she changed handbags. She appeared at the point of tears.

Gabby solved the problem by stopping a passing waitress and asking for a menu—they were disposable printed sheets. When she delivered one, Gabby scrawled her name across it in bold strokes and passed it to Vaughn, who added his own oversized signature.

"This way, you won't forget where you met us." Gabby grinned and handed it back to the woman who was all smiles and soaking in the attention she was getting from everyone around them.

"Is it always like this?" Della asked after the two women had left, still excited and talking over each other. "Having your meals interrupted like that?"

"Comes with the territory," Vaughn told her. "We couldn't do what we do without our fans."

They were saying goodbye outside the restaurant after signing more menus for other people, including the two couples who'd been sitting at their table, when Stephanie threw her arms around Gabby's waist and hugged her. Stunned by the impulsive show of affection, Gabby didn't hesitate to return the girl's embrace.

"I want to be just like you when I grow up," Stephanie said. "I want to be a NASCAR driver and travel all over and win races."

Vaughn wasn't displeased with his daughter's ambition. It was a good life, an exciting life. Funny, though, she'd never said anything about wanting to be a driver before she'd met Gabby. He guessed he ought to thank his impetuous driver for inspiring his daughter and rekindling her old zestful enthusiasm.

CHAPTER ELEVEN

GABBY WAITED until they were on the road before she said anything to her mother, hoping a delay might soften her attitude. It didn't.

"You seem to have left your usual gracious charming self home this evening, Mother. Mind telling me what your problem is?"

"Don't use that tone with me, young lady. I'm still your mother."

Della had mounted her high horse. Gabby waited, saying nothing.

"It's about time you grew up, Gabriella. This flitting from one thing to another is immature and very unattractive."

"Flitting?"

"Aside from the fact that racing cars at ungodly speeds is dangerous and a constant source of worry to me, it's completely inappropriate for a woman. Have you never wondered why there aren't any other women drivers?"

"There are."

"Pshaw." Her mother dismissed the comment with the wave of her bejeweled hand. "You can count them on your fingers."

Gabby wondered how her mother knew that, since she professed to be so ignorant and disdainful of the sport.

"Once upon a time there weren't any women running major corporations, either," Gabby retorted. "Are you planning to resign as CEO of OI and start knitting afghans and canning peaches?"

It was foolish to provoke her mother, but Gabby couldn't help herself. This conversation had been brewing for months, if not years. Maybe it was time to have it out once and for all.

"Is that what all this racing nonsense has taught you, to be smart-mouthed and disrespectful?"

"Mother, I am not a teenager. I'm a grown woman with the right to make my own choices, my own decisions and that's exactly what I'm doing. As for what driving race cars has taught me, it's to stand up for myself. That's what you and Dad always said I should do. Of course, that applies only until I make a decision you don't like. Then all of a sudden I'm some ungrateful, immature adolescent. Respect is a two-way street, Mother. I'd like for you to respect my choices for a change."

"Not when they're foolish, dangerous and self-indulgent."

They'd arrived at Gabby's condo. She was tempted to tell her mother to get in her car and go home. Instead she invited her upstairs for a cup of tea.

The women remained silent until the tea was poured, then they settled down at the table in the kitchen that Gabby rarely used for more than preparing her morning coffee and toast. She couldn't remember the last time she'd even heated a frozen dinner in the microwave, much less cooked a meal.

"Racing isn't foolish, particularly dangerous or self-indulgent, Mother. It's a multimillion-dollar enterprise with tens of millions of followers."

"You can't deny it's dangerous."

"Of course there's an element of danger. That's part of its attraction. Skiing is dangerous. Football is dangerous. Plenty of sports are dangerous."

"You call driving a car a sport?"

"What would you call it? Driving a car at a hundred and eighty miles an hour takes considerable physical and mental concentration and coordination. Every driver I know works out regularly because it takes a lot of strength and stamina to drive a car nonstop for five hundred miles. In case you haven't noticed, Mother, I'm in the best shape I've ever been."

Della grumbled but didn't dispute the point. "It's unladylike."

Gabby shook her head. They'd been over this before. Many times. "I notice you're wearing pants this evening—nice outfit, by the way—not a dress, not a pinafore and a sunbonnet."

She could see her mother was about to snap that one doesn't wear a sunbonnet at night. Gabby wished she would, maybe then they could both have a good laugh and break the tension between them, but they didn't even share the same sense of humor.

"So this is what it's come to," Della continued. "Snide, hurtful comments that disrespect me and do you no credit. Your father and I brought you up to be better."

Here it comes, Gabby thought. The lecture about her rightful place in society.

"You brought me up to be my own person." At least, Dad did. "To think for myself and follow my dreams. Well, my dream is to race stock cars."

"For now," Della shot back. "What happens when this

latest obsession wears thin? Like playing the piano or being a fashion model? What are you going to do then?"

"I don't know," she admitted. It didn't feel like it was ever going to wear thin. "I'll find out when the time comes...if it comes. Right now this is what I want to do, what I feel most alive doing."

"As I said," Della intoned frostily. "Self-indulgent."

Reluctantly, Gabby had to concede that her mother might have a point, but she wasn't about to admit it.

"What's so terrible about my doing what I want to do? I'm not hurting anyone. In fact I'm giving pleasure to millions of fans."

She was tempted to say she was also making a lot of money, but a good deal of it came from O'Farrell sponsorship, so she left that part off.

"You have a more important role in life, Gabby. You're a member of the OI board. You need to take an active interest in the company."

"Why? I'm on the board of directors only because Dad put me there. I didn't ask for it and they don't need my input, which they would probably consider interference, anyway."

"Someday you'll replace me as CEO," Della said. "You can't do that without knowing what's going on."

"That's a mighty big assumption. Has it occurred to you that I may not want to be CEO of O'Farrell Industries?"

"Not be..." Della's lips tightened into a thin line. "Your father took a small furniture manufacturing company and turned it first into a national and then an international retailer of quality home furnishings, and now you...."

"I know what he did, Mother, and I'm enormously

proud of his achievements. But let's not ignore the little detail that he also thoroughly enjoyed what he was doing. Do you really think he could have been so successful if he hadn't? Was he being self-indulgent because he did what he loved doing, what he was good at?"

"And now you're rejecting the legacy of all that dedication and hard work," Della declared in outrage, ignoring the question.

"I'm not rejecting anything." Gabby realized she'd raised her voice. Lowering it, she went on. "Just because he liked being a corporate mogul doesn't mean I want to be."

"His life's work, and you just toss it aside. He must be turning over in his grave."

"More like smiling, Mom."

Della's chin began to quiver. She stood and turned away, stiff-backed. She could play drama queen with the best of them when the circumstances warranted. There was an element of the histrionic now, but Gabby didn't doubt the underlying genuineness of her mother's reaction.

"Dad understood my desire to race cars. Why can't you?"

"Because it's not right." Della enunciated the words slowly, forcefully, her voice muffled by tears. "You're better than that."

"You're right. I'm a better driver than I demonstrated last Sunday, and I intend to prove it. To you. To me. And to Vaughn Steiner. Which brings us back to the original question. Why were you so impolite to him this evening? He did his best to be friendly and you gave him the cold shoulder. You embarrassed me with your bad manners."

It was a shocking statement and a high insult to a woman who prided herself on always knowing which fork to use at dinner. She was also the dowager of diplomatic phrases for alleviating awkward moments at social gatherings—none of which she'd used tonight.

Della placed her hands on the back of the chair she had been sitting in. "I have no intention of encouraging this attraction you have for that man."

"Attraction? Mother, he's my boss."

"Attraction," Della declared flatly, and resumed her seat. "Do you honestly think I didn't notice the way you looked at him. You may call him your boss, but your feelings for him go deeper than that. It's wrong, I tell you. Wrong in so many ways."

Gabby didn't want to believe her mother. Della was confusing respect and admiration, maybe even a kind of hero worship, for something else. Vaughn was an attractive man, but what her mother was suggesting was complete nonsense.

"I hold him responsible for you sinking deeper into this self-indulgent and wholly inappropriate lifestyle," Della declared.

"You haven't listened to a word I've said, have you?"

"As for your attraction to him—"

"I'm not attracted to him, damn it. Not the way you're implying."

"I suggest you think very carefully about getting involved with a man who's impaired."

"Impaired?" Gabby cried. "What the hell are you talking about?"

Della closed her eyes and took in a breath. "Gabriella Lucinda O'Farrell, you know very well what I'm talking about. He can't use his right hand."

"Of course he can," Gabby argued. "You saw him signing autographs. Sure, he's lost some strength and dexterity, but he can still use it."

"He ate with his left hand."

Because his grasp wasn't always firm and sometimes he dropped things. Gabby had seen it happen, seen his embarrassment when it did.

"You make it sound much worse than it is," she told her mother. "There are a lot of left-handed people."

"The fact remains he's handicapped. It may not be very serious now but you heard what the doctor said at dinner the other night. It could get worse. He could lose the use of his hand altogether, of his whole arm."

Gabby felt her inside quiver. Out of outrage? Fear? She didn't like the turn this conversation was taking. She didn't like talking about Vaughn this way.

"Just the opposite. He's getting back more use of it every day."

Was that true? Gabby wasn't sure. Some days she hardly noticed that he had any handicap, but that might be because she'd gotten used to the way he'd learned to do things to compensate for his limitations.

"And what if he doesn't get better?" Gabby asked. "Or even gets worse? What difference does it make?"

Della shook her head, but instead of anger or defiance in her expression, Gabby now saw resigned sadness.

"Brave words, honey. And I'm sure you mean them. People shouldn't judge other people by their disabilities, but they do. I know firsthand what it's like to live with an incapacitated spouse."

Gabby stiffened.

"I loved your father," Della went on, her voice soft and sympathetic. "But living with his handicap wasn't always easy. When he was first diagnosed with MS it didn't seem to make a big difference, but our life together was never the same after he lost the ability to walk. We used to travel, go places, do things. That all changed. We didn't get invited to people's homes, to dinner parties and social gatherings because people didn't know how to deal with a man in a wheelchair. It wasn't just steps. It was the image. He needed help doing things everybody else took for granted. In those last years the business suffered, too."

Gabby had never heard her mother talk about her father this way, which, as far as she was concerned, was to her mother's credit. It shocked her now to learn that these thoughts, these feelings, had even been there. And it offended her.

She'd accused *Gabby* of being self-centered. Did she not realize how selfish she sounded? Sure, Gabby had seen people's reactions to her father's condition, but she always considered it their problem. Did Brock know his wife felt this way?

Gabby's dad had been her greatest champion, her indomitable inspiration. When things went well, he was there to cheer her on, to pat her on the back and tell her how proud he was of her. When they went poorly, he commiserated and helped her find the will and fortitude to do better. Della accused him of spoiling Gabby, and maybe she was right. He'd certainly indulged her in many ways, but then he was the one with the spirit of adventure, with a willingness to try new things—silly things, fun things—simply because they were there.

When Gabby had shown interest in racing, her dad was the one who'd suggested she hire a coach to teach her. After she'd won a few races, it was he who'd encouraged her to push the envelope, to go faster, to be more daring. When she had a chance to compete in the NASCAR Busch Series, he'd arranged for OI to sponsor her—to the tune of a couple of million dollars. An investment, he told the board. One that had paid off handsomely for OI and for her.

Della said they didn't go anywhere after he was wheelchair bound, but that wasn't completely true. He'd gone to as many of Gabby's races as his schedule and energy permitted. It hadn't been easy for him and his heavy motorized wheelchair was certainly an inconvenience, but the NASCAR family had done everything it could to make him welcome, to give him as much access as possible to what was going on, while at the same time making sure he was safe. Too bad her mother had never gone with him. She would have seen him laugh and grin. She'd missed witnessing those last few times when he was happy. Happy and proud of his daughter.

When he died last year dozens of NASCAR drivers and crew members attended his memorial service. Even Della was moved by their support and compassion.

"I'm sorry you have no respect for what I do, and that you seem to hold only contempt and disdain for the people in my life, but that isn't going to change anything, Mother. I'm a race car driver. Get used to it. If I ever give it up—and I seriously doubt I will—it'll be my decision, not one imposed on me by you or anyone else. I would have liked some encouragement and support from you, but I see I'm not going to get it. So let's leave it there. You do your thing, Mom, and I'll do mine."

Della stared at her daughter, took a deep breath and rose from the table.

"You're making a bad decision, Gabriella, but I can see my views mean nothing to you." She moved her chair under the table and left the room.

Gabby followed, watched her mother pick up her handbag and go to the door.

"I wish you could understand, Mom."

Della just shook her head and walked out.

As Gabby washed the two cups and saucers, tears streamed down her face. They'd get over this eventually. Somehow.

CHAPTER TWELVE

VAUGHN SPENT THE WEEKEND in Greensboro. On Saturday morning he took Stephanie shopping at the mall. That afternoon they played miniature golf. His weakened right arm didn't inhibit his performance, but that was because it was all putting. He'd never been an avid golfer, but he'd enjoyed the camaraderie of the links when he found the time and he usually surprised himself and his companions with his low scores. He would definitely have a high handicap now, he thought grimly. He doubted he could hit a ball fifty feet on a driving range.

They attended church the next morning and that afternoon, while Grace stayed home to fix Sunday dinner, he did something he'd never done before. He took Stephanie to a go-cart track.

Vaughn couldn't believe the wonderful feeling it gave him to see his daughter behind the wheel. She had the usual problems the first few rounds. Driving too slow, then too fast. Losing control in the first few turns, inadvertently cutting people off, being cut off, herself. But to his delight—and hers—she figured out how to overcome most of the problems on her own.

When one of the bigger kids tried to wedge in ahead of her, she refused to be intimidated and held her ground, eventually forcing him to back off. Just like her dad.

Vaughn cheered madly. "That's my girl!"

A little while later when she continued to have trouble negotiating a particular right-hand turn, she asked her daddy for advice.

"Pay close attention to what you feel," he told her. "You can tell when you're about to lose traction. The secret is to slow down before that happens, then hit the gas after you're past the halfway point of the turn. If you wait until you begin to slip to put on the brake, it'll be too late."

Stephanie nodded, considering his words. He and Lisa had agreed never to talk down to their daughter. If she didn't understand what she was being told, she could ask for an explanation. In this case, she didn't.

It took her a few more laps before she got the hang of it, but once she did she beat the socks off all the other kids.

She was a bubbling, excited chatterbox on the way home. What amused and worried Vaughn was that she was anxious to tell Gabby all about it. He had to remind her that her grandma would be interested, too.

When they reached home Vaughn began to appreciate his daughter's intuition. Grace was reserved when she was told what Stephanie had been doing. At least, Vaughn noted, Grace didn't say anything negative.

As he was tucking her into bed, Stephanie balked at going to school the next morning.

"Why can't I stay with you and race go-carts again? Please?"

He would have loved to say yes. He recognized and completely understood the child's thrill of getting behind the wheel. For him that intoxicating feeling of power, of defying danger had never gone away. It was the compulsion, what some people called an obsession, that turned men—and women—into race car drivers.

Keeping the girl out of school was out of the question, of course. Still, since he was leaving early Tuesday morning and wouldn't see her again until next Monday, he might have relented if Grandma Grace hadn't been there to play the heavy. Her uncompromising firmness reinforced how grateful he was to her for taking on the role of full-time parent.

And indeed, Tuesday brought him back to his other reality. At sunrise he threw the last remaining articles into his suitcase, kissed his sleeping daughter goodbye and slipped out of the house. He drove to the airport, boarded his private jet and flew to Chicago, the first stop in a chain of stop-and-go meetings over the next two days. He arrived in Las Vegas at noontime on Thursday.

At McCarran International Airport, a chauffeur was waiting to take him directly to the track east of the sprawling city, bypassing Glitter Gulch and the Strip. He'd watched the Entertainment Capital of the World grow over the years and was amazed at its size and diversity. He had the driver drop him off at his RV in the infield.

The stock cars and most of their teams had arrived the day before.

"How are the test runs on 111 going?" he asked Mack Roberts as they strolled through the garage carrying soft drinks in foam-rubber Koozies emblazoned with the team logo. It was only March but the weather in the desert was already warming up.

With no crowds and no one actually on the track at the moment, the place was relatively quiet, compared with what it would be like in a day or two. But the garage area was far from relaxed. The invigorating vibrations of engines being revved and tuned could be felt and heard up and down the line, a teasing prelude to what would follow.

"Good," Mack answered. "The chassis survived unscathed, the power train and engine intact."

Test drivers had already put the car through its paces.

After repairs, a car might appear to be sound but still not function quite the way it had before a wreck. All the components would check out individually, but somehow the combination had lost its magic.

"Is Gabby... Are Gabby and Brett here yet?"

"Brett's due in late this afternoon. He has a couple of guest appearances scheduled at casinos downtown starting at one, but they'll no doubt run overtime. Always do." He chuckled. "He'll probably show up with scratches from fighting off the women." Mack checked his watch. "Gabby should be arriving any minute now."

The two men talked about the condition of the track, strategies for pit stops and who they thought their drivers' chief rivals would be. As always, Jem Nordstrom was at the top of the list of people to watch.

One of the biggest challenges Vaughn had assumed when he organized his teams was keeping out of the way, doing his job and letting others do theirs. This was especially true with regard to Mack. As the senior crew chief, Mack was the guy who coordinated the activities of the two teams, kept track of the details and made sure everything got done right and on time.

Technically the driver was in charge. He—or she—approved modifications and changes, but everybody knew the crew chief was the real power broker, the person who ran the show, including at times, the driver. The owner's main function was to run the business side of the operation, to keep the money flowing and pay the bills. If one of his cars made it to Victory Lane and he wasn't there, someone else could represent him—or no one. That couldn't be said for the crew chief.

Mack had been Vaughn's crew chief when he was driving for Shelby Racing. Convincing him to join this new venture had been a major coup. Vaughn was also well aware that he could lose him if he stepped on his toes. Mack respected him and welcomed his contributions on things that only a driver could know—the feel of a particular track, for instance—but respect was a two-way street.

When Vaughn looked up and saw Gabby walking toward them, he felt a strange lightness in his chest, a euphoria, he realized a moment later, which was completely inappropriate. She was one of his drivers, and he was reacting to her as a woman. The logical side of his brain tried mightily to categorize her as a key member of his team, but his psyche knew better.

Gabby O'Farrell was a woman he'd had dinner with, gotten to talk to about things other than cars and racing. He almost wished now he hadn't.

Almost.

He respected her driving skills and he admired her gumption in taking on a challenge that few people, male or female, dared accept. Until last Friday evening, he'd been able to treat her as a business associate, and he had to continue to treat her that way. Hadn't he given her the same kind of hard time in California he would have given a male driver?

But he'd also seen the softer, more feminine side of her when she talked and laughed with Stephanie. He didn't want to think of her as a woman right now. But the fit of her jeans as they clung to the curves of her hips conspired against him, as did the bright slanting sun, casting her upper torso in tantalizing, distinctively feminine relief.

"Hi," she said when she got within hailing distance. Their eyes met, but she immediately diverted hers to Mack. "What time do we meet?"

"Five," he said.

The Number 111 car rumbled by on its way to the garage stall from the track. With a wave, Mack was gone.

Vaughn turned toward the track. She walked beside him. From behind the pit wall they watched cars zoom by on repair test runs.

"How's Stephanie?" She shouted to be heard above the deafening scream of high-powered, unmuffled engines running full-open. "I really enjoyed meeting her. Cute kid."

"Fine. Sends her regards. Told me driving home she wants to be just like you."

She glanced up at him. "I'm flattered...a little intimidated...never thought of myself as a role model... pretty heavy responsibility."

"You can handle it. How's your mom?"

"Mother is Mother." Gabby watched Number 186, Jem Nordstrom's Chevy, streak by. "I apologize for her rudeness the other night."

"No need to," he said, close to her ear, and caught a whiff of flowers instead of the acrid smell of hot asphalt and scorched rubber. "Besides, she wasn't rude exactly. Don't imagine she's real happy about you driving around in circles at a hundred and eighty miles an hour."

Gabby looked over at him and gave him a twinkling grin. "You've been eavesdropping on our conversations."

"Probably blames me for enticing you into this dangerous foolishness," he added.

She laughed. "You must have my apartment bugged, too!"

Combined with her elusive scent the remark suddenly conjured up images of a bedroom. He couldn't have described any of the details of the room or the bed, but he could easily imagine Gabby on it. In a negligee. Black. With delicate lace along the edges. Transparent enough for him to see…

He shut his eyes and tried to remember what they had been talking about. Racing. Her mother's attitude.

"She's sponsoring you, so she can't be completely opposed to racing."

A pack of three cars streaked by, breaking up Gabby's reply. "That…my father's decision. Dad…much more adventurous."

"Sorry I never met him."

"The two…you would…gotten along fine."

Two more cars shot past, a team pacing each other. The pungent smells of cauterized rubber and acidic exhaust permeated the air.

And something else. A feeling. Companionship? But with tension, like a spring that was both pulling and pushing.

Gabby looked at her watch. "Got to go. Need to check in with my crew." And she was gone.

BRETT WAS LATE getting back from the Strip, so it was closer to five-thirty by the time the meeting with the two teams finally got under way. Just before they sat down, he called Gabby off to the side.

She had to admit he looked damn good in his racing uniform, his thick blond hair curly but neatly trimmed.

"Gabby," he said after one of the mechanics had passed by and was out of earshot, "I want to apologize for last time. I was out of line. It won't happen again. I'm sorry."

"Oh." She was stunned. She'd never expected the big jerk to actually own up. His contrition left her feeling guilty for misjudging him. Still, she couldn't very well tell him it was all right, because it wasn't. He'd scared her, though she'd never admit it to him or anyone else. "Apology accepted. And thanks."

"I hope we can be friends." He held up his hands, palms out. "No strings attached. Just friends."

"I'd like that." She smiled. "No strings attached."

"And maybe we can help each other out on the track."

Uh-oh. Was this a ploy? Manipulation to get her help?

Before she could respond, Mack called them to take their seats. He waited until they'd quieted down, then, as prearranged, asked Vaughn to lead off since he was familiar with the track as a driver.

"This is a D-shaped track like Daytona," Vaughn said, nodding to the large graphic on display, "but shorter. A mile and a half. Only one real straightaway and two lesser ones. You'll be spending a lot of time in fairly shallow turns. Banking runs from a nearly flat three degrees on the long backstretch to a max of twelve degrees in the turns. The front stretch is canted nine degrees. Those aren't real steep banks, which means you're going to have plenty of opportunities to spin out."

He looked from Gabby to Brett, who were sitting in the front row next to each other.

"No restrictor plates here."

Restrictor plates, which reduced airflow into the carburetor to limit speed, were mandated at Daytona and Talladega, because the longer length of the tracks would otherwise allow cars to reach unsafe speeds, and safety was top priority in a sport that was by its very nature dangerous.

"Here the short track and straightaway will automatically limit your speed. That means you have to take advantage of every opportunity to get ahead of the competition. Team up as much as possible. Draft each other, when you can. Keep talking to your spotters. Make sure you know the field."

Drivers had very limited visibility. Their cars were all the same size, which meant that, except for the leader, the forward field of vision was restricted by what they could see between the cars in front of them. Keeping track of the other forty-two vehicles was impossible, so they depended on spotters up in the bleachers to tell them what was happening behind and ahead of them. The spotter also negotiated alliances of convenience with other spotters and drivers to gain temporary advantages. This centered primarily on drafting, either in pairs or sometimes in longer chains.

"What about offers from Nordstrom's spotter?" Phil Rickover, Gabby's spotter asked.

"Pass," Vaughn said without hesitation, only then glancing at Lacey Dillers, Brett's crew chief, who nodded agreement.

"I can promise you," Vaughn went on, "Nordstrom is still hot under the collar about California. Also, forget about making any offers to him. He'll see it as a sign of weakness and use it to screw you. We're all in this to win, but when it gets personal, it gets particularly dangerous."

Drawing on his experience and having learned from his failure to pass on a valuable lesson to Gabby, Vaughn talked about some of the other drivers, how they handled themselves in various situations, in shallow versus sharp curves, whether they were likely to honor a deal.

They then discussed the next day's qualifying round. Each car ran a single lap and was precisely timed electronically. The car that was the fastest got the pole position, the inside position in the first row. The second fastest was on his right, the third behind the first and so on, forming a double column of cars, number forty-three being by himself at the very end. The last car was not necessarily the slowest, however. Alteration to a vehicle after qualifying, violation of a rule or a variety of other contingencies could—and often did—put a driver at the end of the lineup.

Saturday they'd have designated times to practice on the track. They wouldn't be alone, however. Other cars would be there doing the same thing; the numbers would just be limited and they wouldn't be competing against each other. That didn't lower the tension, though. Members of other teams would be watching. Performance in trials could influence tactics in the races that followed.

Everyone knew their jobs. Meeting adjourned.

On Friday, Brett qualified for sixth place. Gabby came in twenty-ninth.

"Not bad," Vaughn told Brett late Friday afternoon. "Your big job early in the race will be to hold on to that position."

Vaughn watched Gabby. Clearly she wasn't happy about being so far back in the pack. She'd expected to do better, and frankly, so had he. It wasn't necessarily her, however. Her restored car might still need some fine tuning.

The engine team would be checking into that this evening. They wouldn't be allowed to change components or make any modifications to the engine or the vehicle without incurring penalties, but they could still fine-tune what was there. Sometimes the merest quarter turn of an adjustable screw made all the difference.

The important thing for Gabby was that she'd qualified. She was in Sunday's race.

It amazed him how much he wanted her to win.

CHAPTER THIRTEEN

BY THE FOURTEENTH LAP, Gabby had nosed up six positions. By the twenty-third, she'd gained another seven, putting her in sixteenth place. The short track and the limited straightaways made Vegas a special challenge. Jem Nordstrom had started in fourth position, then dropped back three when he had a lousy pit stop, but he was still ahead of her.

In the thirty-fourth lap she came up behind Freddie Harris in the Number 107 car.

"Offer a draft," Gabby told her spotter. She wasn't sure if Freddie would trust her after the fiasco in California, but when they'd been at the infield care center after the spin-out, he'd been philosophical about it.

Clem Dawson came up behind her and made the same offer. Within seconds the three of them were cruising by four other cars on the outside, one of them driven by Jem. And just ahead of him was Brett who'd slipped two places after his last pit stop.

Freddie became suddenly vulnerable to being boxed in and split off. The snake line broke. Gabby was again on her own. But not for long.

Brett appeared in her rearview mirror, pulled up tight on her tail and together they eased past two other cars. Then he saw a break and sling-shotted to the inside and was abreast of her.

They began playing leapfrog at a hundred and eighty-five miles an hour.

She sat on his rear bumper for two laps. They moved up one more position and found themselves behind Chet Tuney, who had the lead. According to Gabby's spotter, Tuney was ripe for a pit stop. Still, the three of them dominated the field for the next four laps, until Tuney was forced to pull off onto pit road.

That put Brett in the number one position. Gabby stayed glued to his bumper, offering him the extra push of a draft to establish more distance from the pack. Two more laps. Brett gained extra points for laps lead.

They came up on the rear of the trailing pack. Kermit Ferrell was in the race to finish, not to win. He inched right, giving Brett access to the inside. Gabby shot forward with him.

Suddenly, Gabby was rocked, thumped, her grip on the steering wheel instinctively tightening to steel.

Expletive, expletive, expletive.

She'd shredded a tire.

She muttered another bad word. Plural bad words.

Fortunately pit road was close. Eyes in the rearview mirror, she steered the wobbling car inside the shoulder line and limped to her place on pit road.

The team did its job with skill and speed. She was back on the track within fourteen seconds, but the unscheduled stop cost her dearly. Twice after that she got boxed in, once by Jem.

She finished eleventh. Brett had come in fourth, his best showing to date.

VAUGHN DIDN'T hang around. After congratulating his drivers for their good showings, voicing his approval of the way they'd teamed up with each other, he had his chauffeur take him directly to the airport. He wasn't a gambler or a drinker and he was too tired to enjoy one of the Strip's legendary shows. Besides, he was well enough known that someone was bound to recognize him, and he wasn't in the mood for people tonight. He also didn't want to take a chance on someone seeing him in a casino, among blackjack tables and roulette wheels. The last thing he needed was a reputation as a high roller.

Sitting alone in his private jet on the flight home he reviewed the day's events. He couldn't complain about the way things had gone. A win would have been better, no question about that, but there was something to be said for a slow build up to victory. The joy of anticipation. The excitement of unpredictable competition.

He could have stayed for the night's celebrations. It would have been interesting to see Gabby let her hair down, figuratively speaking, but he was beginning to think spending too much time with her was a bad idea, a distraction he didn't need.

What he did need was to spend more time with his daughter. Last weekend had given him a taste of the family life he and Lisa had shared. He owed it to Stephanie to make her life as whole as he possibly could.

With the change in time zones, it was after midnight when he finally pulled into his driveway in Greensboro. He'd called Grace hours earlier to let her know he was coming and had told her to go on to bed. He wasn't surprised, however, when he found her waiting for him, the TV volume turned low, knitting needles in hand.

"How's Steph?" he asked after greeting her and getting a cold beer from the kitchen.

"She was glad to hear you were coming home tonight. Insisted she was going to wait up for you. I suggested she put on her jammies and read in bed." Grace smiled. "The sandman won out hours ago."

Vaughn chuckled. "I got to thinking on the way home. There's something I need to talk to you about."

"HOW WOULD YOU like to go to the race in Atlanta this weekend?" Vaughn asked his daughter the next morning. He was drinking coffee and nibbling on an English muffin as she scarfed down cold cereal.

Her eyes grew as round as the circles of banana slices floating in her bowl of milk.

"Really? I can go to the race with you? Like me and Mom used to?"

"Yep." He noticed she was able to mention her mother this time without tearing up. Progress. "But only if you want to. If you would rather stay here—"

"I want to. Yes. Yes. I want to."

Vaughn loved seeing the old excitement in his daughter. "Grandma said she'll talk to your teacher about getting you out of school early on Friday. You'll probably have extra homework, but the two of you can drive down to Atlanta and meet me there."

"Yippee." She jumped off her chair and ran around to his side of the table. Throwing her arms across his chest she said, "I love you, Daddy."

"I love you, too, sweetheart." He gave her a hug and a kiss on the top of her head. "Now you better finish your breakfast or you'll be late for school."

He wanted to tell her a few seconds later not to eat so fast, but all he could do was smile to hide the lump in his throat.

"LET'S NOT TELL Daddy about the truck," Grace said Friday evening as they pulled onto the infield at the Atlanta race track. "We don't want him to worry."

"Okay." Stephanie pointed to the massive RV on the left. "There it is."

Grace halted in front of a thirty-six-footer, still shaking from the near miss they'd had on the interstate near Stockbridge, just south of Atlanta. Big-city traffic always made her nervous. She'd been tooling along in the middle lane, careful not to exceed the speed limit, when a car on her left shot across her lane for an exit on the right. Startled, she'd naturally slammed on her brakes, only to jump nearly out of her skin when the trucker who had been tailgating her blasted his horn. The next thing she heard was the screech of brakes as the eighteen-wheeler loomed in her rearview mirror, blocking all the light as it closed in on her bumper. In total panic she'd stomped on the gas pedal. Fortunately the lane in front of her was open for several car lengths, but even then she nearly crashed into the little Geo she shot up behind.

Somehow—she still wasn't sure how—she'd managed to get over to the right lane and eventually pull onto the shoulder of the road and stop. Her hands, her whole body, shaking so violently, so painfully, she'd been afraid she was having a heart attack. Sitting beside her, Steph had turned stiff and white. Concern for her granddaughter finally forced Grace to breathe, to calm herself down. The two of them had hugged each other tight for several seconds, while the Crown Victoria sat buffeted by the wind sheer of cars and trucks whizzing past. After they'd both calmed down, Grace coasted slowly, still on the shoulder of the road, to the exit a few hundred yards ahead. She stayed on the service road the rest of the way.

The memory of their close call still made her feel sick. She just hoped Steph didn't inadvertently blurt something to her father. Vaughn wouldn't be pleased if he found out, and this time he might actually take action.

Grace's driving record wasn't exactly spotless. She'd been involved in several accidents over the years, totaling one car a couple of years ago, though it really hadn't been her fault, regardless of what the police report said. And that fender-bender on Wycliff Road a few months ago? Well, it hadn't been her fault, either. She hadn't been the one who'd run the stop sign. The guy in the Toyota had, even though he denied it.

Vaughn didn't need to worry. No one had been hurt in any of those incidents and no one had been hurt today. She certainly didn't want him feeling he had to restrict her driving, and she was certain he would, if he found out. She suspected he was already concerned about her driving, because he'd offered a couple of months ago to pay for a limousine service to take her wherever she needed to go. To make things easier for her, he'd said. But that was silly. If she thought for one minute that she couldn't handle a car… Well, she could…just fine.

She'd hardly turned off the ignition when the RV door flew open and Vaughn leaped down the steps. Stephanie ran to him with open arms. He gathered her up, gave her a great big hug and swung her around, supporting her weight with his left arm.

"I wondered when you were going to get here," he said, giving his daughter a loud, sloppy kiss.

He smiled over at Grace, who was climbing out of the car, a little unsteady on her feet. "How was the trip down? Run into any problems?"

"Traffic was heavy," she said.

He lowered Stephanie to her feet. "Have you eaten already? Is that why you're late?"

"We talked about it," Grace answered, "but both of us just wanted to get here."

"Daddy, I'm hungry."

"Well, I know just the place. Really good ribs and chicken."

"Hey, I thought I heard a familiar voice."

They turned to see Gabby, all smiles, standing at the corner of the coach. She was wearing slim-fitted chinos and a blue T-shirt with the NASCAR logo emblazoned across the chest.

Vaughn tried to not stare.

"Your dad said you were coming in tonight," she said. "Welcome to Atlanta."

Stephanie ran to her. Gabby crouched and they gave each other a big hug. Grace pursed her lips. She'd never received that kind of reception.

"Grace, this is Gabby O'Farrell." To Gabby, Vaughn said, "This is Grace Wilcox, Stephanie's grandmother."

Gabby rose and extended her hand past the clinging girl. "I'm very glad to meet you, Grace. Steph has told me so much about you." The two women shook briefly.

"We're going to get some barbecue," Vaughn said. "Care to join us?"

"Please," Stephanie begged, looking up with pleading eyes.

Gabby gazed at her, hands gently resting on her back. She smiled.

"If I'm not interfering with family time," she said to Vaughn.

"You're not," Stephanie said without hesitation.

The barbecue turned out to be every bit as good as Vaughn had promised, with just enough tang to it. During the meal, Grace concentrated on the group dynamics. Stephanie was clearly infatuated with Gabby, hanging on to her every word, puffing up whenever Gabby gave her a compliment, which she did often.

Vaughn's reaction, while different, wasn't hard to read, either. Infatuation might not be the right word, but he was certainly attracted to her. Grudgingly, Grace understood why.

Gabby O'Farrell was much prettier in person than in the pictures Stephanie had shown her in magazines. In those impromptu race track shots her hair was always sweat-plastered against her head or windblown, her face inevitably smudged with grease and road grime.

The woman sitting across from her now had a beautiful complexion. If she was wearing makeup, other than a subtle lipstick, it was so expertly applied as to be virtually invisible. And even in casual pants and a T-shirt, it was obvious this woman was sophisticated. Grace knew from the articles she'd read that Gabby was from old money, but she would have been able to figure that out on her own.

Seated on Vaughn's right at the picnic-style table in the busy restaurant, there was familiarity in the way Gabby touched his hand when she enthusiastically approved his taking Steph to the go-cart track. He tried not to show it, but Grace could see Vaughn's awareness of her touch and the desire in his eyes for it to continue.

As far as Grace knew, he'd never been unfaithful to

Lisa, and he'd been respectful of her memory since her death. But Grace didn't consider herself naive.

Since Rob's death when Lisa was fifteen, there hadn't been any other man in her life. Having Lisa to care for had been enough. But she knew men had needs. Rob had taught her that much. How Vaughn satisfied his was something she chose not to think about.

But what she saw flowing between him and this rich, worldly, female driver was more than mere lust, and it scared her.

CHAPTER FOURTEEN

THE FOLLOWING FRIDAY evening Gabby was reminded of the adage to be careful what you wished for when her mother showed up at her motor coach.

She was dressed in a gray wool gabardine pantsuit with a white polka-dotted dark blue silk blouse and low-heel silver sandals. The outfit might have looked elegantly casual on the set for a TV interview, but at the Atlanta race track it was about as appropriate as steak at a wine and cheese party.

"What are you doing here, Mother? How did you get through security?" Gabby blurted before her brain had a chance to temper her surprise. But, of course, Della O'Farrell was a sponsor, so getting a pass was no problem. Probably had the race track manager to personally escort her here.

"Now, there's a pleasant welcome." Della stepped across the threshold. Strangely she didn't seem to take offense at the ungracious greeting and at least gave the impression that the acrimony of their last parting was all but forgotten. Forgiven might be another matter.

She surveyed the interior of the immense RV, gave occasional nods of approval. She should. This home away from home was worth over a million bucks.

"Very nice," she said as she took in the stainless steel appliances, refrigerator, freezer and wall-mounted double ovens. "I don't suppose you have room here for me."

"There's just one bedroom, but the couch folds out and I'm told it's actually quite comfortable." To Gabby's knowledge her mother had never slept on a sofa bed in her life, and she didn't suppose she was about to establish a precedent now. At least Gabby hoped she wasn't.

"That's all right," Della said. "I have a suite reserved at the Hyatt in Atlanta." About twenty-five miles away. That should be far enough.

"I'm sure you'll be much more comfortable there." Gabby grinned. "I know the room service is better."

Della ran her hand along the salmon-colored marble kitchen counter. "Is someone already staying with you?"

How gauche of you to ask, Mother. "No one is staying with me." *Not that it's any of your business.* "You didn't answer my question. What are you doing here? You've never come to a race before."

Della's answer was distracted as she peered up at the skylight over the cooking island. "I thought it was time I did, since you seem so determined to pursue this…"

"Inappropriate lifestyle?"

"Let's not get into all that again, Gabriella. At least, not now."

"Actually, I'm glad you've come, Mother. Maybe getting to see a race firsthand, you'll begin to understand the excitement and why I'm so in love with what I'm doing."

Fat chance, Gabby concluded, based on the scowl on her mother's face.

"Did you drive yourself?" she asked.

"I hired a car and driver. I could have asked Keenan to

bring me—" he was her regular chauffeur during the week, mostly to and from work "—but he has family visiting this weekend and I didn't want to take him away."

"I wish you'd told me you were coming. I could have set up a schedule for you to meet people, tour facilities. As things stand right now, I won't have much time to spend with you. In fact," she looked at the digital clock over the stovetop "there's a meeting in about twenty minutes that will probably take awhile. I have an idea, though. You remember Stephanie, Vaughn's little girl. She and her grandmother are staying with him in the coach next door. Why don't we go over there? I'll introduce you, and the three of you can keep each other company while we're gone."

"Vaughn lives right next door? My, isn't that convenient."

Gabby wanted to explode, but it wouldn't do any good. Probably only make matters worse. Protesting too much, her mother would say. On a sigh, she went to the door and opened it. "Shall we?"

Her knock at the neighboring coach brought an immediate response. Vaughn opened the door wide.

"Gab—" he started, then realized who was standing at her side. "Della! What a pleasant surprise. Gabby didn't tell me you were coming." He stepped aside, inviting them in. Della entered first.

"I didn't know myself," Gabby said, giving him a mild shrug to answer the unspoken but very obvious question in his eyes: what is she doing here? "Mom is just full of surprises. Unfortunate timing, though, since we have a meeting in a couple of minutes. I thought I'd bring her over here to visit while we're gone."

"Good idea."

Stephanie moved up and stood beside Gabby, her shoulder in contact with her hip. Without prompting she said, "Hello, Mrs. O'Farrell."

"Hello, Stephanie. I didn't realize you were going to be here, too."

"Grandma brought me."

Vaughn introduced his mother-in-law. The two older women shook hands perfunctorily.

"Can I go over to my friend Cindy's?" Stephanie asked. Freddie Harris's motor coach was parked two spots down. He and his wife had four kids. Cindy was the youngest and the same age as Stephanie. "Her daddy bought her a puppy and she said I could come over and play with it."

Grace answered. "If you go anywhere else, be sure to call me. I want to know where you are."

"Okay." The girl called a general goodbye and was out the door.

"I'm sorry to have to leave you so soon," Vaughn said, "but we have a strategy meeting in a few minutes. Probably take about two hours. If Stephanie returns before we do, why don't the three of you go ahead and eat? Gabby and I can grab something on our own later." He turned to Della. "I'm very happy you've come, Della. I hope you enjoy the weekend. If there's anything we can do to make you more comfortable, to answer questions or show you around, please don't hesitate to ask."

Outside, he and Gabby walked toward the hauler where their meeting was to be held. The roar of engines being tested and tuned was already intense. The ground trembled and the air vibrated with the excitement that surrounded every race.

"This is your mother's first time at a NASCAR race, isn't it?" he asked.

"Dad used to come to my Busch races whenever he could, but Mom was never interested."

They reached the hauler but stopped outside.

"Am I reading this wrong, Gabby, or is there a little bit of tension between the two of you?"

Gabby gave him a rueful smile. "You're seeing us at our worst, I'm afraid. On most things we actually get along fine. At least we used to. I'm beginning to see a different side of my mother since Dad died."

"Well, she's your corporate sponsor now, so we'll do our best to take good care of her." He glanced over at her troubled expression. "I promise."

"I know you will." Gabby mounted the high steps into the hauler. "I just hope she appreciates it."

"WE SEEM TO have been abandoned," Grace said when the two women were alone. "You drink tea?"

Della placed her purse on the black-slate countertop between the kitchen and the dining area. This coach was every bit as luxurious as Gabby's, though it was more masculine in character. "I'd love a cup."

"Green or black?"

"Black, please."

"I have Darjeeling, English breakfast and Earl Grey."

"Oh, Earl Grey. Definitely Earl Grey."

"Good," Grace said as she opened the teak cabinet beside the gas stove. "It's my favorite, too."

Della shifted her weight onto a stool on the other side of the work space.

"Your granddaughter is a lovely child," she remarked.

"So polite and well-mannered. Very refreshing these days. Did she tell you Gabriella and I had dinner with her and her father at that Japanese steak house in Greensboro?"

Grace checked the water level in the kettle and lit the propane burner under it. "That's all she talked about for days. Mostly about Gabby and how she wants to be just like her when she grows up. Your daughter is very nice, Mrs. O'Farrell, but until that evening I'd never heard Stephanie say anything about wanting to be a race car driver."

"To be honest, Gabby has other…better qualities I'd like to see your granddaughter emulate. And please call me Della. The truth is, I'm not pleased with Gabby racing cars, and if we're going to be completely candid, I'm not thrilled with her infatuation with your son-in-law, either."

Grace put out tea cups, a sugar bowl and lemon slices she removed from the refrigerator. "Vaughn's a good man, Della."

"I have no reason to think he isn't. I meant no offense. When we first met at the PR sponsorship signing, he was completely professional and I must say quite charming, and at the restaurant the other night he gave the impression of being a good father. It's clear his little girl adores him. What concerns me is his encouraging Gabby in this racing nonsense. It's fine for a man, I suppose. They need their toys, but to be honest, Gabriella is capable of more and better."

Della realized she was being less than tactful, if the other woman was a dedicated fan. But her instincts told her she wasn't.

The water boiled.

"Gabby has told me about your daughter," Della said as Grace poured the water. "I'm terribly sorry. To lose a child… well, you can understand how I worry about Gabriella."

"My husband died some years ago. Lisa was our only child. I'm so grateful to Vaughn for inviting me to live with him and Stephanie. If I didn't have her now, I don't know what I would do. Let's sit at the table, we'll be more comfortable there."

The two women carried their steaming cups from the counter to the dining area that made up one end of the living space.

"I'm not happy about what's developing between Vaughn and Gabby, either," Grace admitted. "I don't like Lisa being replaced so easily and so quickly. I'm afraid Stephanie will forget her."

Della nodded sympathetically.

"And I don't want my daughter to continue with this racing business. Gabriella has other responsibilities she needs to take seriously."

Grace smiled over the rim of her steaming tea cup. "Sounds to me, Della, like we're in complete agreement. For different reasons, but that's all right. The question is, what are we going to do about it?"

CHAPTER FIFTEEN

VAUGHN CORRALLED Felicity Mayhew, his public relations rep's assistant, later that evening and gave her her marching orders.

"Fel, you have Steiner Racing's number-one job this weekend. I want you to squire Della O'Farrell around, introduce her to track and race officials, take her wherever she wants to go, answer her questions, do whatever is required to make her happy, and above all, make her fall in love with NASCAR racing."

The attractive young woman was perfectly suited to the challenge. Not only was Felicity knowledgeable about NASCAR as only a diehard fan could be, she was well-educated and well-spoken. Vaughn hoped that as a female she would also know just how to connect with another woman.

"She's never been to a Busch or NEXTEL Series race, so don't assume she understands what's going on. Be prepared to explain even the most basic details in uncomplicated terms, without making her feel self-conscious."

"Just leave her to me," Felicity responded.

In the pit area the next day Vaughn saw Felicity animatedly talking with Della who was wearing a headset. He doubted the older woman understood much of the chatter she overheard between drivers, team members and spotters, but there was no mistaking the rapt expression on her face as she strained to decipher what was going on or the satisfaction in her eyes when she did.

Vaughn gave Felicity a thumbs-up.

Gabby ran a good race on Sunday, one of her best. She led six laps, earning points and she paired off with Brett on several laps, sometimes to her advantage, just as often to his. Their early friction seemed all but forgotten and they were working together as a team. Scuttlebutt offered two explanations for Brett's attitude adjustment. One was that Lacey Dillers, his fifty-year-old crew chief, had gotten wind of the private discussion between him and Vaughn and had followed it up with an ass-chewing of his own. The other was that Brett had found a new girlfriend. Either reason was feasible. Vaughn suspected it might be a combination of the two.

Gabby came in fourth, her best showing to date. Everyone was ecstatic. Even Della cheered and held up a fist in approval of her daughter's performance.

Then Vaughn did something really stupid.

While the crowds in the stands were cheering for Jem Nordstrom, the day's winner, as he rode his victory lap and drove into Victory Lane, Gabby pulled into the pit area where her team chief, the crew, Vaughn and her mother were waiting. She crawled through the window, stood on the ground, removed her helmet, shook out her short, now sweaty hair, raised her arm in acknowledgment of her applause and beamed a radiant smile.

Impulsively, Vaughn grabbed her around the waist and planted a kiss on her mouth. The crowd around them hooted, whistled and cheered.

The moment he felt her lips make contact with his he knew he'd made a big mistake. Team owners didn't kiss their drivers. Not on the mouth. Not in front of her mother. He just prayed nobody had gotten a picture of it. Exuberance. That's all it was. Exuberance. But people didn't like simple, innocent explanations. He thought about Brett's earlier retort. *You're not fooling anyone. Everyone can see the way you look at her.*

Fighting to recover equilibrium, he released her abruptly in what felt like a transparent attempt to minimize the significance of what had just happened. He stepped back and laughed, grateful when a reporter shoved a microphone in his face and asked him about the race.

He extolled Gabby's driving skills in the just-ended race and, hoping he wasn't making an even bigger mistake, sought to further diffuse the situation by inviting Della, who was standing a few feet away, to comment on her daughter's good showing.

He had to hand it to the woman. Without missing a beat she praised Gabby to the sky, then proceeded to congratulate everyone on the Steiner team for their professionalism and achievements. She thanked the Atlanta race track folks for their generous hospitality and willingness to answer her sometimes naive questions. Best of all, she acknowledged she was finally beginning to understand and appreciate the allure of racing, though, she admitted with a laugh, she still found it a bit loud. For someone who professed ignorance about NASCAR racing, she managed to hit all the right notes.

All well and good, but…

Vaughn hadn't missed the expression on her face as he'd released her daughter. The benevolence that had been growing over the past two days seemed to vanish in the heartbeat of that single kiss. Her reservations now weren't so much against racing but about him personally.

When the gathering crowd finally dissipated and the crew dispersed to their tasks, Vaughn wanted to leave with them. He'd acted on impulse and wrecked what should have been triumph in winning the support of their biggest sponsor. But Della called his name and came toward him, Gabby at her side.

"I'm leaving," she said, "but before I go I want to thank you personally for being so generous with your time and hospitality. I have to admit this has all been somewhat overwhelming, but you've given me an insight into what really happens at races, more than I would have gotten watching it on television or sitting in the stands."

The words were appropriate, kind, even gracious, but he couldn't help feeling there was a less amicable subtext in them.

"I'm so glad you could join us," he said, "and that you enjoyed yourself. I hope you'll come back again soon and often. You're always welcome. If you ever have any questions, please don't hesitate to call me."

They shook hands.

"I must run," she said a moment later. "I understand traffic is going to be quite heavy. Please give my best to Grace. I enjoyed meeting her. And Stephanie, of course. She's a delightful child."

"I'll walk you to your car," Gabby said. Did he see distress in her eyes? Was it at him or her mother?

Vaughn watched them disappear among the after-race crowd streaming through the garage area. He should be worried about the damage he'd done by kissing Gabby, and he was, but catching fleeting glimpses of the sway of her hips as she maneuvered around people, all he could think about was the alive feeling he'd experienced when he'd held her in his arms and the titillating sensation of her lips against his.

Kissing Gabby had definitely been a mistake, a big mistake, not because he didn't enjoy it, or even because he did, but because Della O'Farrell had seen that he did.

ORDERED CHAOS REIGNED over the next few hours. The two stock cars were loaded into their haulers. Tools were inventoried and packed up. Worn tires, used engine oil and lubricants were properly disposed of. The garage area was cleared and cleaned. The majority of team members headed for home. The five-hundred-mile race in Tennessee wasn't for two weeks—their last two-week break in the nine-month-long season—so a few people decided to hang around until morning before moving on. Most of them ended up at the Sway Bar, a local honky-tonk for an evening of music and relaxation.

Gabby had just gotten out of the shower and was drying herself off when her cell phone rang.

"Hi, Gabby." It was Stephanie. "Daddy is making me go to bed now. I'm not tired, but he says I should be. Can you come over and tuck me in? Please?"

A dozen images ran through Gabby's mind. Sitting at the side of the little girl's bed, smoothing out her sheet and blanket, and pressing an affectionate kiss on her forehead. They all had a definite appeal, but she also wondered how Vaughn and Grace felt about it.

"What do your dad and grandmother say?"

"It's okay, if it'll get me to go to bed. I'm not sleepy at

all. Maybe you can read me a story. Mommy always read to me before I went to sleep."

Uh-oh. She was treading on sacred ground here.

"I'll be over in a couple of minutes, honey."

Gabby had been planning on going to the Sway Bar for a while, so she put on her jeans and red-plaid Western shirt.

"I'm sorry Stephanie bothered you," Grace said, meeting her at the door, "but she can be so insistent sometimes. And she knows how to wrap her father around her little finger."

"My mother will tell you I did the same thing with my dad."

"She had no right to bother you."

"I don't mind. Really."

But the thin line of Grace's mouth indicated she did. Turning stiffly, she led Gabby to Stephanie's room.

Vaughn was there, sitting on the side of the bed, reading *Rumpelstiltskin.* He turned his head at Gabby's entrance and stopped reading.

"Thanks for coming."

"Gabby, Gabby," Stephanie called out. "Will you finish reading to me?"

Vaughn reached out and offered her the book, the place held with his index finger. She slipped hers in under his and felt the warmth of his hand touching hers.

Leaning over, he kissed his daughter on the forehead. "Just the one story now, pumpkin, then I want you to go to sleep."

"Okay, Daddy."

He rose from the bed. "Thanks for doing this," he murmured in Gabby's ear—there was that scent again, but stronger this time, more intimate, more alluring. He walked to the door and left the room.

Gabby assumed his place on the side of the bed—the spot was still warm.

"You ran a near perfect race today," the girl told her. "That's what Daddy said. I watched the whole thing. You were awesome."

He hadn't said that to her, but she'd felt it, the way he looked at her. And of course the kiss. Her mother hadn't said a word about it. She didn't have to. Gabby knew her well enough to read the body language. She was furious about it, but Gabby didn't care. She'd enjoyed it.

"I didn't win, though," she told Stephanie, "or finish in the top three."

"Daddy says it doesn't matter. You showed your stuff and earned plenty of points."

Gabby had to smile. "Showed my stuff, huh?" She wondered what else he'd said—or thought. "Well, he should know. Now, let's get to this story so you can go to sleep."

"But I'm not sleepy," the kid insisted, even though she could hardly keep her eyes open. Gabby smiled, knowing the battle would soon be lost.

It was. Long before Gabby got to the happily-ever-after, the little girl was deep in dreamland.

She kissed her on the forehead, turned off the bedside lamp—there was a night-light in an outlet on the other side of the room—and tiptoed out.

"Don't close the door all the way," Grace said softly. She came forward and adjusted it so there was an inch between it and the jamb.

"Thanks for coming over," Vaughn said, his eyes roaming the length of her. "You look like you're ready to party."

"I was on my way to the Sway Bar when Steph called."

"I was thinking of stopping by there, myself. Why don't I drive?" He turned to Grace. "You don't mind, do you?"

She made the right sounds, but Gabby could see his mother-in-law wasn't thrilled by the idea of them going out together. Gabby also sensed that Vaughn was unaware of the negative vibes she was putting out.

THE DANCE HALL was packed. A few drivers, a lot of team members, and as they soon found out, even more fans. Within minutes of their arrival they were swamped by people telling Vaughn how much they used to enjoy watching him race and asking if he'd be racing again. He gave noncommittal answers. They recognized Gabby, too, and congratulated her on her fourth place. Then came the requests for autographs. They signed books, odd scraps of paper, beer coasters, a T-shirt or two, even a few dollar bills.

But they also got to dance. Gabby soon discovered that Vaughn Steiner was remarkably smooth and graceful on his feet. She also found the closeness of his lean body against her in the slow numbers tantalizing.

Back away, a stern voice inside her head cautioned. But then another one—the same little smiling whisper that had gotten her into trouble repeatedly in the past—urged, *Go for it, honey. Let's see what happens next.*

She and Vaughn stayed until nearly midnight and might have remained longer, but he had already told her he was driving back to Greensboro in the morning with Stephanie and Grace because he needed to spend more time with his daughter and a car trip was a great opportunity to talk and sing. Gabby herself had fond memories of car trips with her dad when she was a kid, before he got sick. Singing songs, playing games and sometimes just sitting in silence in the warm security of his company.

She needed to get up early, too. She was flying back home but had several stops along the way for guest appearances at auto-parts stores and an interview at a local television station.

Vaughn parked his pickup next to Grace's Crown Victoria and came around to Gabby's side of the truck, just as she was getting out.

"I'll walk you home," he said.

She chuckled. "It's hardly twenty-five yards, Vaughn."

"Still, there might be a snake under the steps."

She grinned wider. "You think?"

"You never know. Or lions or tigers or bears."

"Oh, my. I didn't realize Georgia was so wild and dangerous."

"You can never be too careful."

They strolled around the front of her motor coach and turned the corner to the platform that led to her door.

He followed her up the steps and stood there as she twisted the key in the lock. She pushed it open, immediately went to the security alarm panel and punched in the code.

Turning around, she asked, "Would you like to come in?"

He was standing in the doorway. After a moment's consideration he stepped inside, but only beyond the threshold, not completely into the room.

"Come here," he said quietly, the request somewhere between an order and an invitation.

Without thinking she obeyed.

He reached out and placed his hands on her hips. "Thank you for a wonderful evening."

Then he slipped his hands behind her back, lowered his head and kissed her on the lips.

A kiss unlike the one he'd given her earlier in the day. That one had been a spontaneous act of exuberance. This invoked a different kind of passion.

She responded in the only way she could by wrapping her arms around his waist and colluded in the assault on her senses.

The little voice inside her head said, *So this is what happens next. Aren't you glad you said yes?*

CHAPTER SIXTEEN

"SINCE WE'RE GOING to the park," Gabby said, as she loaded her contribution to the afternoon's excursion in the back of the Vaughn's Explorer, "I brought along tennis rackets just in case we want to play."

The call had come the following Sunday afternoon as she was catching up on her laundry.

"Gabby, can you come to the park for a picnic with me and Daddy tomorrow? I don't have to go to school."

Only an optimist would plan a picnic in the last week of March, but why not? She was sure Vaughn would have a Plan B.

Stephanie sounded nearly out of breath with excitement, but Gabby could also hear the girl's worry that she would say no.

She reviewed her schedule. One of her infrequent appointments with her hairdresser in the morning. A luncheon with Glenna Holbrook, her PR manager. A few routine chores after that. She'd been looking forward to a workout at the health club later in the afternoon, then maybe going for a few laps in the heated swimming pool.

"Sounds like a wonderful idea, kiddo." She'd eat lightly at lunch and put off the other things until Tuesday and Wednesday. "Just tell me where and when and what I can bring."

"I've never played tennis," Stephanie said now, as they buckled up in their seats. Gabby had left her Mustang parked at the curb.

"Never?" She feigned astonishment. "I figured you for a regular tennis star."

"Me?" But it was easy to see the child was pleased at the notion.

"I brought a racket that's just your size. Would you like to try it? It's really not very difficult."

Vaughn groaned, a sly grin playing on his face.

"Ever played?" she asked him.

"I experimented a few times in high school. Never got past the frustration stage. Being made a fool of by a fuzzy little ball doesn't do much for a guy's ego. I found full-contact sports like football and wrestling a lot more satisfying."

She could imagine him in shoulder pads and helmet, though the image of him scrambling on a mat in shorts and skimpy tank top was even more intriguing.

"You probably didn't have the right instructor," she opined. "Nothing to it, really."

He sucked in his cheeks. "Just like stock car racing, huh?"

She had to smile. "Exactly. Except that instead of driving around in circles you hit a ball back and forth over a net."

He sighed wistfully. "And to think champions get paid millions of dollars for doing something so simple."

"Simple doesn't always mean easy."

"Amen to that."

They pulled into the paved lot at the public park and unloaded their stuff. Stephanie wanted to carry her racket, so Gabby also gave her the bag with several tubes of tennis balls, while she grabbed the other rackets and her Tupperware container of potato salad. Vaughn tossed a red-plaid blanket over his right shoulder and lugged the cooler with his left hand.

They found a spot within sight of the ball courts and set up their picnic site. Stephanie jumped up and down impatiently.

"Will you teach me to play tennis now, Gabby? Will you?"

"If it's all right with your dad."

She looked pleadingly up at her father. "Is it?"

He couldn't have said no even if he'd wanted to. "Sure. I'll sit over here and watch."

"Don't you want to join us?" Gabby asked. "I brought another adult racket. You could team up with Steph."

UNCONSCIOUSLY Vaughn flexed his right hand. Would he be even capably of swinging a racket? Certainly not with any speed or power and he doubted with any accuracy. He'd learned he was most pain free when he avoided strenuous use of his right arm and hand. Quick repetitive motions, especially those that resulted in any sort of impact, like using a hammer, were the worst.

Play left-handed? In the past two years he'd learned to do a lot of things with his left hand. Why not tennis? And this would be another activity he could share with Steph.

"Okay, let's give it a shot."

They strolled to the deserted tennis courts.

"We'll start off easy," Gabby said, "with the basics."

First she instructed Stephanie on how to hold the racket, how to swing it with full arm extended and how to make even contact with the ball.

Nice legs, Vaughn noted, when he should have been

concentrating on her instructions. Smooth and evenly tanned. He wondered when she got the time to sunbathe. But that was only a passing thought. His interest was stirred by the play of her calf and thigh muscles as she bobbed and weaved on the balls of her feet. Then there were the bewitching contortions of her upper body as she swayed and twisted.

She had been bouncing balls to Stephanie, who either missed them or sent them off in erratic directions. Suddenly, Gabby popped one over to him. It streaked by without his even raising his racket.

"Daydreaming?" she asked with a smile.

"Uh, sorry," he muttered, and loped off to retrieve the ball.

Shamed into getting his mind to override his libido, he realized that, in addition to being elegant in her movements, she was also a darn good teacher. Gabby patiently helped Stephanie adjust her movements until she got it right, constantly adding positive comments. Stephanie was also a quick study, but then her time in the go-cart had already demonstrated that.

He had no trouble returning the soft volleys Gabby started sending his way and, to his own amazement, looked forward to the challenge of a full court. He felt self-conscious, though, of his right arm. Flexing muscles to keep the elbow bent and his hand at waist level, which would have been the normal stance, was taxing, so he tended to let it hang at his side. He kept watching to see Gabby's reaction, but she displayed none.

"Okay, now let's see if you can get the ball over the net," she said to Stephanie. "You're going to have to hit it really hard."

Stephanie's initial attempts were predictable failures.

The first three balls she actually connected with dribbled under the net. The next two went into it.

"That's better," Gabby assured her. "Now a little higher."

The next one popped over the wire and would have been out of bounds, but that wasn't important at this point.

"Wow. You're doing great, Steph," Gabby observed. "I don't think I've ever seen anyone pick tennis up so fast."

She served a ball to Vaughn at moderate speed. He was relieved when he was able to return it with reasonable accuracy, but the real pleasure was watching her stretch to connect with it.

They batted the ball back and forth for another half hour. Soft balls to Stephanie. With increasing velocity to Vaughn. If the ball got to Gabby's side of the court, she expertly lobbed it back in a slow, gentle arc that placed it exactly where her pupil needed it to be.

Then, as if a switch had been turned off, Vaughn saw Stephanie wilt with fatigue.

"Hey, girls," he called, "I don't know about you, but I'm getting hungry."

"Me, too." Stephanie brightened. "Can we eat now?"

"I thought I was the only one who was starving." Gabby gathered up the balls on her side of the court. "Let's go."

"Not bad," she told Vaughn as they made their way back to the picnic area, "for a guy who hasn't played since high school."

"As you said," he replied with a broad grin, "it just takes the right teacher."

"I LIKE YOUR potato salad better than Grandma's," Stephanie said as she forked up another mouthful from the mound on her plastic plate. "She puts pickles in hers. Yuck."

"I thought you liked Grandma's potato salad," Vaughn said. "You certainly eat enough of it when she makes it."

"It's okay," the girl conceded, "but I like Gabby's better."

"Please don't tell your grandmother that," Gabby urged. "You would hurt her feelings. Mine is different, that's all. I don't think any two people make potato salad exactly the same way. Besides, sometimes I put sweet pickle relish in mine, too."

"You do?"

Gabby nodded. "Yep. It gives it a nice tang. I didn't this time because I was out and didn't have time to run to the store to buy more."

"Well, I still like yours better," Stephanie insisted, and took another bite.

Even though there were several concrete picnic tables nearby, Stephanie wanted to spread the red-plaid blanket on the lawn and sit cross-legged on it. They ate Grace's fried chicken, Gabby's potato salad and the peach cobbler Stephanie had helped her grandmother make earlier that day. Lately, Vaughn and Stephanie had been going out to dinner alone on Monday nights while Grace played bridge with friends from church.

Turning this Monday's supper into a picnic and inviting Gabby had been Stephanie's idea. Vaughn hadn't objected in the least, but since it was turning into a special occasion, he'd felt obligated to invite Grace along.

"You know Monday is my bridge night," she'd replied tersely. "And so does Steph."

It had been Grace's idea that he take his daughter out to dinner every Monday, so they could be together. And it had been her idea to use the time to be with her friends. Surely she wasn't jealous of Gabby. There was no need to be. At least none he could see.

"I've got something for you," Gabby told Stephanie.

The girl's eyes widened. "What is it?"

"Since you couldn't join us in Las Vegas, I thought I'd bring you a souvenir." She reached into the side pocket of her tote bag and removed a box, which she handed to the girl. "I understand you don't have a charm bracelet."

Stephanie fumbled excitedly to open the present. Inside she found a silver bracelet with a single charm in the shape of a diamond-studded horseshoe.

"Daddy, look." She held out the box for him to inspect. "I want to put it on."

He lifted it from its bed of white cotton. "This is really special."

"I figured you could get a charm from each of the places where NASCAR races," Gabby explained.

"What a wonderful idea," Vaughn said, making warm eye contact with her. "Thank you."

Stephanie bubbled with a second thank-you, jumped up and danced around, holding out her wrist with the bracelet on it.

"That was a nice thing to do," he told Gabby.

"It's nothing much. I just thought she'd enjoy it."

"You must let me return the favor. How about dinner Thursday night after the team meeting? I know a great little place up in the Tennessee hills that serves the best mountain trout you've ever tasted."

Gabby watched Stephanie skipping around a few yards away and imagined a rustic mountain cabin, candlelight, a roaring fire in a big stone fireplace. "You're on."

CHAPTER SEVENTEEN

BUT HE WASN'T.

They arrived at Bristol on Thursday afternoon only to learn that the Number 111 car was experiencing engine problems, so the evening was spent test-driving modifications and sharing pizza with the crew.

Gabby qualified for thirty-eighth position the next day and came in a face-saving seventeenth on Sunday.

At the race at Martinsville the following weekend, sponsor commitments again kept her and Vaughn from the quiet, intimate dinner he'd promised. She came in a disappointing twenty-third, the only consolation being that Brett managed to beat Jem Nordstrom out of tenth place.

Gabby's fortunes improved in Texas, where she finished fifth, but again other duties denied them the privacy they craved.

"Next week," Vaughn promised. "I know a great little out-of-the-way Mexican restaurant in Phoenix."

"I'M STILL RUNNING loose," Gabby said into her microphone.

"Let's try a wedge," Mack said.

They'd adjusted the tire pressure twice so far, but the Phoenix track had odd turns that were shallow banked and Gabby was having trouble maintaining rear-wheel traction.

"Can you hold out till the next pit stop? Or do you need to come in now?"

She wasn't due for a gas-and-go for another ten laps.

"I'm good," she said.

It meant she would have to be extra sensitive to the car's stability and more cautious in the turns. She hated not being able to ram the pedal to the firewall at will. It was all a calculation. Would the time she'd lose in a pit stop exceed the fractions of a second she might have to sacrifice on the track? Having to hold back at all was nerve-racking.

She was in eighth place with one hundred and fifty laps to go. Brett was six cars behind her, Jem Nordstrom four. The three of them had been neck-and-neck most of the race, each gaining the advantage over the other for a lap or two, losing it, resurging and slipping back again. More than once she and Jem had been in a position to help each other, but neither had even bothered to make an offer. He had accepted an offer to draft from Brett early in the race, only to take advantage of it and screw him. Brett had sworn it wouldn't happen again. Maybe the pundits were right. Nordstrom was out to get Vaughn and anyone on his team.

Gabby pressed hard on the inside of Turn Four, started to break halfway through and was forced to slip to the outside to regain control. She gave up her position in the process. After a blue streak of unladylike words, she announced she was coming in.

"What am I doing wrong?" she asked Vaughn in utter frustration as she glided to her stall.

"I don't think it's you," he said through the headset.

"I'm putting in a wedge on your outside rear—" Mack broke in "—and taking three pounds from the tire."

"It may be the track," Vaughn said. "Neil Mullins says Duke Jones is having the same problem."

The right side of the car bounced onto the pavement.

"Go. Go. Go. Go. Go."

In Turn One she pushed Number 111 as hard as she could.

"Any better?" Mack asked.

"I think so. We'll see on Turn Two."

Five seconds later she shouted into the mike, "Yes."

She pushed harder. "Where am I?"

"Tenth. Jem is three ahead of you."

"Here goes."

She rammed her right foot to the floor, passed Tate Cummings on the outside of the backstretch and Brian Rule on the inside of the next turn.

Brett separated her from Jem. She got on his tail and the two of them drafted past Jem. But it didn't last. Brett miscalculated the duo in front of him and suddenly found himself boxed in. Gabby wanted to shunt around him on the outside, but Jem was there holding her captive. They held that pattern for the next eight laps.

They were down to the last six now and fighting for fourth place. If she could move out ahead of Jem, she had a chance for third and there was still barely enough time to move up another two places.

It didn't happen. Jem refused to give an inch. Well, under the circumstances she wouldn't have, either, so she could hardly hold that against him, but it was frustrating as hell. She was running perfect, but too late.

She came in fifth, right behind Nordstrom. She couldn't see his face, but she did see his fist rise in an arrogant gesture, one finger extended.

The expression on Vaughn's face when she got back to

the pit mirrored her own frustration. He complimented her on running a good race and commiserated with her on the disappointing outcome. It left them both unsatisfied.

THE TEAMS PACKED UP the stock cars, their tools and personal belongings. Many of them left that evening for home and family or to move on to the site of the next race. Talladega, Alabama.

Vaughn invited Gabby to his coach to say goodbye to Stephanie and her grandmother before he put them on his jet to fly them back to Greensboro. The night before, over dinner in Vaughn's coach, Gabby had given Stephanie a new charm, this one in the shape of Arizona's famous saguaro cactus.

Vaughn was staying in Arizona for another two days to work out business details with a couple of sponsors headquartered in Phoenix and Tucson. He would get back home for only one night this week, but he was determined to spend as much time with his daughter as he could. Her attitude and behavior had much improved over the past few months. Partly he knew it was because she was getting to spend time with him at the track and they were spending more time together when he was home, but he was convinced Gabby had contributed a good deal to Stephanie's improved outlook, as well. Grace furnished stability, discipline and essential affection, but Gabby connected with the child on an emotional level.

"Will you be at the school on Wednesday like you promised?" Stephanie asked her.

"You bet. Three o'clock. I have it on my calendar. I'm looking forward to seeing you dance."

"Oh, okay." She brightened. "I'm a wood fairy."

"I can't wait." Gabby bent and kissed the child on the cheek. "You take good care of Grandma now. Make sure she eats her carrots."

The girl giggled, then leaned forward and whispered, "She hates carrots."

"I do not," Grace objected. "They're just not my favorite."

Gabby feigned shock, then looked up at Grace and winked.

"But she still makes me eat mine," Stephanie went on.

"'Cause they're good for you. For her, too." Gabby lowered her voice dramatically. "So make sure she eats her share."

Stephanie grinned. "Okay."

Grace clicked her tongue before giving in to a grudging smile.

At the girl's insistence, Gabby rode out with them to the private ramp where Vaughn's Learjet was parked.

"I promised you a Mexican dinner," he reminded her after the plane was airborne.

"Can I take a rain check, Vaughn? I'm really not in the mood for crowds this evening."

As big as the Phoenix metropolitan area was, there was a good chance one or both of them would be recognized by NASCAR fans no matter where they went, which meant their dinner would be interrupted at least once, probably more often.

"You must be hungry, though," he noted. When she didn't argue with him, he added, "Look, the place I had in mind isn't far from here. How about I call them and see if they'll put together a couple of take-out meals?"

"Sounds good to me," she said.

He used his cell phone, got information, put in the call

and twenty minutes later they picked up a chimichanga and a gordita. The restaurant owner threw in sopapillas and honey for dessert.

They returned to Gabby's motor coach, where she transferred the food from the containers to china plates and substituted silverware for the plastic utensils that had come with the food.

She accessed her TiVo and they sat next to each other on the couch.

Between bites of food they discussed different aspects of the race, analyzing the tactics and idiosyncrasies of various drivers. She repeatedly asked him what he would have done under particular circumstances, how he would have reacted. Watching the screen, she saw where she had missed an opportunity or two, but he was quick to point out that she had no way of knowing about them at the time unless her spotter alerted her. He hadn't. Still Vaughn wasn't ready to judge the guy too critically. There were enough Monday-morning quarterbacks.

She split a honey-dipped sopapilla with him, then in a move that seemed automatic and perfectly natural, settled against him in the crook of his right shoulder.

Apparently unaware of the effect she was having on him, Gabby pointed out various things on the screen. He tried to concentrate on the pictures flashing in front of him, but her warmth and her scent kept short-circuiting the process.

He may have lost strength in his right arm, but he sure hadn't lost feeling, and he was still able to stroke his hand along the smooth skin of her forearm.

In her excitement over the race, her body bounced and rubbed against him. The soft friction of her thigh against his, of her side against his rib cage, began to stimulate an inevitable response.

She asked him a question. At least he thought she did, but he had no idea what it was. Receiving no reply, she turned her head and gazed up at him. Their eyes met and the sound of engines revving was drowned out by the beat of his heart pulsing in his ears.

Her closeness was too much. He couldn't resist the temptation any longer. He lowered his head, turned hers to face him and slowly brought his lips to hers.

OH, THIS KISS was definitely a toe curler.

She should have been shocked, she realized, but she wasn't. She should have resisted, but she didn't. The sensation of his lips on hers sent vibrations through her system unlike any she'd experienced before. She'd wanted this to happen for a long time, ever since that first exuberant kiss in Atlanta and that second more calculated one later that evening. She'd wondered why he hadn't kissed her again and if the next time would be as enticing.

Now she knew.

She fanned her hand across his chest and felt the rapid tripping of his heart. Their lips parted, but only for a second. All at once they were plunging into an even deeper kiss.

His left hand swept up her arm, across her shoulder. It touched the soft flesh beneath her ear. She felt her heart begin to pound in anticipation of the pleasures his erotic explorations promised.

"Gabby," he murmured as their hands and fingers roamed over sensitized flesh.

His lips and tongue traced their way along her jaw, down her throat to her collarbone.

He whispered her name again before mating his lips with hers.

Then, without warning, he pulled back.

"What's wrong?"

He untangled himself and climbed to his feet. "I shouldn't have done that. I had no right."

"Vaughn…"

He moved stiffly to the door, like a man in pain.

"I'm sorry," he said, and before she knew it, he was gone.

She sat where she was for a solid three minutes, then crumpled into the buttery soft leather sofa cushion. What had she done wrong?

Why was he sorry? And about what? That he wanted her? That she had made it clear she wanted him?

Why had he rejected her?

CHAPTER EIGHTEEN

"COME ON. COME ON. Come on," Vaughn muttered as he stood atop the hauler and watched Gabby lead the pack through Turn Two, Brett snug up against her rear bumper. "Come on. Come on. Come on."

The last lap.

Vaughn was shaking his fists, his whole body rigid. Jem was three car lengths behind them and fighting Freddie for third place. Not enough time for either of them to catch up with the leaders, though, unless something went wrong.

Into Turn Three. Gabby hugging the inside of the track, Brett right behind her, giving her a draft.

Don't get greedy, Brett. Don't try to pass. Stay behind her.

They screamed through Turn Four, screamed into the home stretch.

Hang in there. Hang in there.

The checkered flag danced a figure eight. The crowd went wild.

Victory.

Gabby first. Brett second. It didn't get any better than this.

Cheers rang out around him. Vaughn's heart was pounding so hard he thought it would explode.

Gabby had just won her first NASCAR NEXTEL race. His team had chalked up their first victories.

Holy jumping Jehoshaphat!

Before he understood what was happening, Mack Johnson was thumping him on the back and Lacey Dillers had thrown his arms around him in a bear hug. Team members were giving each other high-fives. The stands were going wild. Gabby O'Farrell had won, the first woman driver to win a NASCAR NEXTEL race at Talladega.

All eyes were focused on Number 111, as the other cars pulled off onto pit road. The track was hers now. Gabby owned it. She drove her victory lap. Alone. In the middle of the hot pavement. She had her left hand out the window, waving to the crowd, which was making more noise than the cars that had so recently given it their all.

Brett pulled into the pit, all smiles, as hands reached out to congratulate him. Mustn't forget number two.

Vaughn went to him, shouted hosannas. Brett climbed through the window and jumped to the ground.

"If you kiss me, I'll slug you," he said as Vaughn approached with open arms.

Vaughn laughed and gave the guy a rib-crushing bear hug anyway. Close to his ear he said, "You proved you're not only a winning driver but a team player, Brett. I'm damn proud of you."

They both turned as a new cheer rang out from the stands. Having completed her celebratory lap, Gabby was doing wheelies in front of the stands, sending up billowing clouds of blue-white smoke and the acrid smell of burning rubber while her left hand punched the air.

Pit road was lined with drivers, teams and spectators eager to touch her hand, slap her car and offer more applause. Face beaming, she coasted slowly to Victory Lane.

It wasn't really a lane but a location where she stopped

the car. Vaughn could see she was bursting with excitement, but she couldn't get out of the car until the live TV cameras were ready for her. Some moments just couldn't be missed. The winning driver extricating herself from her car was one of them.

Finally, with all the cameras in place and rolling, she was given the signal and crawled through the window opening. Removing her helmet and raising it high above her head, she acknowledged the adulation of the crowd.

A heady feeling, Vaughn reflected, that single, precious moment when you knew you were the best, king—or in this case, queen—of the racing world.

As she beamed and pirouetted in place, laughing and almost crying, the world she'd conquered came to pay homage. Vaughn and Mack, the pit crew and the guys who worked behind them. NASCAR officials. Track officials. Sponsor representatives. Public relations people. And, of course, the media. Every one of them smiling.

If life was hectic before, that was all mere prelude to what was yet in store for her. Given a hand...make that hands...up, she climbed onto the roof of the car and was handed a magnum of champagne, the cork already set to pop. She thumbed it off and sprayed everyone with bubbly. Holding up the foam-bearded bottle, she flashed another smile, or was it a continuation of the one that had never left her face?

Hands were extended to help her down. More congratulations. Vaughn was one of those waiting for her. They shook hands. Their eyes met. A kiss would definitely have been better, but not here, not in front of the entire world. Not when there was a chance the kiss might linger.

She inched down the line of well-wishers, exchanged compliments, offered thanks to Mack and the team, to anybody else who happened to be in her path, whether she knew them or not. Brett was among them, and when she saw him she didn't hesitate to throw her arms around his neck and give him a great big, loud kiss on the lips. Shocked and delighted, he beamed at her as if he'd just won the grand prize. The masses around them cheered.

The media moved in. TV first. Then radio. Her words were broadcast to the restless, adoring crowd. After that, endless photo sessions. With the team. With the owner. With her many team sponsors. With race sponsors. With track officials. With the car manufacturer's reps.

Vaughn retreated into the background. This was her time, the first of many victories, he hoped. The joy would never grow old or be taken for granted, but nothing quite compared with the exhilaration of the first time, either.

She would be tied up for hours now, giving interviews, posing for pictures. Her face muscles would ache from all the smiling, but the smile wouldn't fade…

IT WAS ALMOST eleven o'clock when Vaughn knocked on the door of Gabby's coach. He'd been waiting, watching for her to come home.

Then she was standing there in the doorway, backlit by the room behind her, her silhouette uniquely hers, her features in shadow.

"Hi," she said, happiness still bubbly in her voice.

"Hi."

"Why didn't you come with us to the party?" She sounded disappointed.

"This was your night. You didn't need a fifth wheel."

"More like a steering wheel." She took a step back and invited him in with a wave of her hand.

"Besides," he said, entering, more nervous than he had reason to be, "I had other things to do. We need to exploit this opportunity."

She closed the door behind him.

He turned. "I've been working the phones, making calls."

"That's great." She stood there, smiling happily, self-consciously. He could feel the tension radiating off her, feel the magnetic pull between them.

"Would you like something to drink?" she asked. "I've got beer and soft drinks. A couple of bottles of champagne, too, if you'd like some of that."

"No. No, thanks. I just came by to let you know what's going on and…" He should leave. It was late. She must be tired. All that excitement today. It had to be exhausting. "And to congratulate you again. You did a great job out there, Gabby."

She shifted, trying to be casual, yet her eyes, as intensely blue as the desert sun at high noon, were searching his, as if she were expecting more.

"I couldn't have done it without you," she said.

"Remember California?"

She snickered softly. "How can I forget?"

He felt intoxicated by her smile. "Remember what I said when you got eliminated, that it was all on your head because you were the one behind the wheel?"

Her eyes twinkled. "Yeah, I remember."

"Same thing applies today. You won the race, Gabby. You were the one driving the car. Other people contributed, gave you the tools, but it was you behind the wheel." He placed his hands on her shoulders. That was safe, wasn't it? "I'm incredibly proud of you."

No, it wasn't safe, he realized when it was already too

late. He was too close, close enough to drown in the scent that was uniquely her. And like any drowning man, he reached out. He dragged her into his arms, held her there. Then he kissed her.

He hadn't planned to—well, not consciously, actively—but that didn't mean he hadn't been thinking about it, dreaming about it.

He kissed her, and she kissed him back.

Last time he'd backed away. This time… He wasn't sure he possessed the strength to do that again—or the will.

He tightened his embrace and deepened the kiss. She coiled her arms around his neck.

"Don't leave me," she murmured a minute later. She laid her cheek on his shoulder. "Don't leave me tonight."

"Are you sure?" he asked.

She gazed up at him. "I'm sure, Vaughn. I'm very sure."

CHAPTER NINETEEN

OVER THE NEXT FEW WEEKS sponsorship offers came to Steiner Racing, but to Vaughn's amazement the big ones were mostly for Brett. There was no doubt the rookie had appeal, especially to the women in the audience. He was young and handsome, well-spoken and, to Vaughn's relief, had turned out to be a good team player. And yes, he had a new girlfriend, a tall, striking redhead the camera adored.

Why the same sponsorship offers weren't coming forward for Gabby was baffling. She was beautiful. She was smart. She had personality that captured both male and female fans. Yet, except for a few small sponsors and a handful that had to be turned down because they were inappropriate for the NASCAR image, she was largely ignored.

Vaughn didn't have a clue as to why she was being shunned and his questions of potential sponsors only elicited vague responses, the most common being that she already had a major, family owned underwriter. That was true, of course, but every sponsor was vulnerable to competitive bids.

Then he saw a sidebar to an article in a magazine about Gabby as the first woman driver to win at Talladega. The reporter had also interviewed Gabby's mother after the big win.

Della expressed great pride that her daughter had won the race and that she had set a new standard for women in doing so. Then she was quoted as adding, "Gabby has always done well at everything she's attempted. That's something her father and I instilled in her from her earliest years. If you're going to do something, work hard at it and do it well. She's never disappointed us. This is another feather in her cap of achievements, something else she'll be able to look back on all her life with a sense of accomplishment."

"It sounds," the interviewer said, "like you don't expect her to continue on with NASCAR?"

"Whether she does or not is of course her decision. Gabby's excelled in so many things over the years that I sometimes tease her about what she's going to do when she grows up."

Zing.

Vaughn wondered if Della might have been misquoted or the comment taken out of context. He'd fallen victim to that a time or two and had learned to be very judicious in his choice of words. Having less direct personal experience with the media, Della may not have been as cautious.

"It's something she would say," Gabby remarked later that afternoon when Vaughn showed her the article. "Mom's very accomplished at left-handed compliments."

"It's hurting you. After I read this I called several perspective sponsors and asked them about it, and they admitted the real reason they've hesitated to make you big offers is that the word is out that you won't be sticking with it. Rumor has it that your father sponsored you because no one else would."

Gabby closed her eyes and clamped her jaw before muttering, "Damn." She took a breath. "You can tell them," she informed Vaughn, "that I have no intention of quitting anytime soon. Not for the next twenty or thirty years, anyway."

He put his hand on her forearms, felt the soft skin, the taut muscles beneath it and gently massaged. "I don't think they need that long a commitment, but I'll pass the information on. It might be a good idea if in your next news conference you made your career aspirations a matter of public record, too."

It would have been nice if that news conference had come after another win, but the races that followed weren't nearly as successful.

She came in eighth at Darlington and twenty-sixth in Charlotte. Vaughn couldn't blame her for the poor showing. Engine trouble had slowed her in the opening phase of the race, and the carburetor adjustment it required had cost her precious laps and put her at the end of the pack. By the close of the race, she'd moved up fifteen places—several cars had been eliminated by then—but she'd run out of time to maneuver her way farther forward.

The result was disappointing, but Vaughn was far from unhappy with her performance. She'd fought like the devil in spite of the odds being against her. To him that counted for a lot. He just hoped fans and potential sponsors saw it that way, too.

A WOMAN in the NASCAR NEXTEL Series was enough of a rarity that the media naturally focused on Gabby.

One magazine put her on their cover and crowned her the Tiger Woods of NASCAR. Sports reporters, even those who weren't her personal fans, inevitably commented on where Gabby O'Farrell had finished at the end of each race, how many points she had accumulated to date and where she stood in the lineup leading to the NASCAR NEXTEL Cup. She was holding her own in spite of having been eliminated at Daytona due to a pileup caused by Jem Nordstrom.

It came as a shock, therefore, when Vaughn received a letter from the CEO of O'Farrell Industries, that the corporation would not be continuing its sponsorship of Gabby O'Farrell in the coming season.

He stared at the paper as if it were some kind of foreign object. It didn't make sense. Gabby was one of the most popular drivers on the circuit. The campaign to assure fans and supporters that she was in for the long haul was beginning to pay off, and she was picking up more secondary sponsors. She was constantly receiving new requests for media interviews and guest appearances, was featured or prominently mentioned in just about every article being published about the current NASCAR season.

"The recent downturn in profits has prompted a careful reevaluation of our current promotional programs," the letter read. "As a result, the board has decided that the large sum of tight advertising dollars currently dedicated to NASCAR sponsorship needs to be radically restructured and the resulting smaller overall expenditure allocated to a broader spectrum of product advertising venues."

It was signed "Della O'Farrell, President and Chief Operating Officer, O'Farrell Industries."

A variety of thoughts stampeded through Vaughn's brain, but he stifled them as he picked up the phone and hit the speed dial.

"Morning, Vaughn," Gabby said when she answered, no

doubt recognizing his name from her caller ID. "How are you this bright sunny Monday morning?"

"Where are you?"

He could picture her holding the telephone away from her ear at his sharp tone, sharper than he'd intended.

"On my way to a radio interview here in town."

"What are your plans for lunch?"

"Is this an invitation? We've never done lunch before."

They'd done dinner several times, and at the end of the evening he'd always seen her to wherever she was staying. Inevitably their good-night kiss at her door led to an invitation for him to come inside.

"A nooner sounds like fun," she said in a light tone.

He couldn't argue that. "I need to see you."

His voice must have again betrayed him, because her next question wasn't playful. "What's wrong?"

"We need to talk, Gabby, but not on the phone. Remember that place we talked about that night in Dover?"

A moment passed in silence. He could picture her face animated with thought.

"The one a mile down the road from the barbecue stand?" she asked.

"Can you meet me there at twelve-thirty?"

"Yes, but can you at least give me a hint about what's going on? Nobody's hurt or anything?"

"Nothing like that. Everyone's fine. I'll see you at twelve-thirty."

After he hung up he contacted his lawyer and financial manager, told them he was faxing a copy of Della's letter and asked for an analysis of its impact within twenty-four hours, as well as any recommendations they might have on how to mitigate its effects.

CHAPTER TWENTY

GABBY SIGNED HER NAME across the bottom of the small poster one of the women at the radio station asked her to autograph right after her on-air interview.

"You're really an inspiration," the woman said. "My daughter is only eleven, but already she's decided she wants to race. Her father isn't very happy about it right now, but he'll come around. He always does where she's concerned."

Gabby thanked her and, as quickly as she could before someone else caught her, made for the exit to the parking lot. She had forty-five minutes to get to the restaurant Vaughn had referred to. Plenty of time. But what was he being so secretive about?

She realized she was assuming it was bad news. It could just as easily be good news, couldn't it?

No, she decided, the tension in his voice wasn't from joy, but concern. Car trouble? Not likely. They had a backup car, backup engine and mechanics who were as good as anyone in the business. Number 111 had been running fine last Sunday. Not a squeak or a sputter. Besides, she didn't get involved in those kinds of decisions.

She arrived at the restaurant fifteen minutes early and was surprised to find Vaughn already there. Several people recognized her and greeted her like an old friend as she passed by on her way to the booth at the far end of the long narrow dining room. She would have liked to sit next to him, but there were too many people watching. She would have liked to greet him with a kiss, too, but that was even more out of the question.

"Hi," she said brightly. "Been waiting long?"

"About five minutes."

The hostess who'd seated her placed a menu on the table in front of her and took her drink order.

"Okay, what's up? You sounded worried on the phone."

"I am."

A waitress delivered a glass of sweet tea and asked if they were ready to order their food.

Gabby wasn't really hungry, not when Vaughn seemed to be in such a funk.

"I'll have the grilled shrimp salad," she told the waitress without even looking at the menu in front of her. "With the green peppercorn dressing." Vaughn requested the same.

The moment the waitress left, Gabby repeated her question. He removed a copy of the letter from the attaché case on the seat beside him.

"Do you know anything about this?" he asked as he handed it over.

She read it, felt her pulse accelerate and read it a second time. "Son of a bitch."

"I guess that means no."

She shot him daggers with her eyes. "You're damn right it means no. What the hell do you think—"

His hand reached out and covered hers. "Calm down, Gabby. I wasn't accusing you of anything. I was just asking a question."

"That's not the way it sounded to me. Why the hell would you think I knew anything about this and wouldn't tell you?"

"I thought your mother might have mentioned something that maybe you didn't take seriously at the time."

"No." She rocked her head back and forth. "She never said a damn thing to me about this. If she'd even hinted she was considering—" She willed her heart to slow its tattoo. "She doesn't like me racing. She's made that clear enough, especially since Dad died. But I never expected this. Damn!"

"If she is so opposed to what you're doing, why is she sponsoring you at all?"

"It wasn't her decision. Dad got the board to approve my sponsorship before he died. The idea never occurred to me that she would cancel it. Damn. I should have realized she'd pull a stunt like this."

"Is the company really doing that poorly? OI's gotten an awful lot of exposure from NASCAR and NASCAR fans are notoriously loyal to sponsors. I should think with you driving, their sales would have gone up over the past year."

The food arrived. It smelled wonderful, but Gabby had no appetite for it.

"I'm on the board," she said, mechanically picking up her fork. "I attended one meeting after Dad died and haven't been to another since. Besides being dull, they meet on Thursdays when I'm not in town. The truth is I hardly even look at the quarterly financial reports I receive, much less the monthly updates." She stared into space. "I guess that's been a mistake."

Vaughn toyed with his salad before biting into a large shrimp.

"What are you going to do?" she asked.

"Find ten million dollars if I want to continue running two cars next season."

"Which means if you can't, you'll have to choose between Brett and me."

He chewed and swallowed before answering. "I don't know how I would do that, except maybe to announce that whoever came out higher in the final standings for the season would stay. But that wouldn't be fair, either."

She forked up a piece of char-grilled shrimp and suspended it over the plate. "No more unfair than tossing a coin, which seems to be the only other alternative. At least this way I can influence where I come out for the year."

They nibbled in silence.

"Telexco is backing Brett," Vaughn finally said. "Maybe I can convince them to back you, as well."

"In the meantime—" she stabbed a chunk of lettuce "—I'm definitely going to have a little conversation with dear Mom."

DELLA LOOKED UP from her desk. "I wondered if you might have forgotten how to find this place. Oh, stop looking at me that way. I won't pretend not to know why you're here. I guess I finally got your attention."

"Is that what this is all about, Mother, getting my attention?"

"In part." She picked up her phone, pressed a button. "Tea or coffee?" she asked Gabby.

Ever the gracious hostess, even when she was stabbing her daughter in the back. Gabby groaned.

"Coffee." At least it would give her something to do with

her hands. The danger otherwise was that she'd be tempted to wring her mother's neck.

"Bonnie, bring us coffee, please." Della put down the receiver and motioned Gabby to the chair in front of the desk.

"Okay—" Gabby slipped into the seat "—you've made your point. You've got my attention. You can rescind your threat to drop my sponsorship now."

Della shook her head. "Oh, we're still going through with that."

"For heaven's sake, Mother. Why?"

The secretary, a slender, middle-aged woman with salt-and-pepper hair pulled back in a bun and wearing a dark blue pin-striped straight skirt and white blouse that could have been right out of the 1940s, entered the room pushing a tea cart on which sat a silver tray. She positioned it at the end of her boss's highly polished desk, one that Gabby's great-grandfather had made by hand a hundred years ago.

"Thank you, Bonnie." Della rose. "I'll take care of it from here."

The woman nodded and left the room.

Della poured steaming aromatic coffee from the silver pot into two Limoges cups and handed one of them, black, to her daughter. Using tongs she put a single sugar cube in the other, added a few drops of cream from a small, matching bone china pitcher, stirred it with a silver spoon and carried the cup and saucer to her place behind the desk.

"Why are you dropping my sponsorship?" Gabby asked, trying to sound objective, businesslike, when what she really wanted to do was to scream the question while pounding on the desk. A year earlier she might have at least raised her voice, but she'd taken a lesson from Vaughn's playbook. Quiet intensity was more intimidating, although she wasn't sure it would work on her mother.

Della sipped her coffee. "If you'd come to any of our board meetings or read the financial reports you've been sent, you'd know profits have been declining."

Last night Gabby had spent hours going over those reports. Her mother was right, sales were up but profits were slipping. The question was why. Other companies were showing higher profits on higher revenue. Gabby had a couple of theories, but until she discussed them with more knowledgeable people, she thought it best to keep them to herself.

"Are you blaming me for flagging profits?"

Della huffed. "Not directly."

"What does that mean?"

"Gabby, your sponsorship in NASCAR has cost us ten million dollars this year, that's more than twice what your sponsorship in the Busch Series cost us the previous two years combined."

"It's a deductible business expense."

"I'm well aware of that. I also know that it's millions of dollars that could have been in the profit column."

"Sales are up. The loyalty of NASCAR fans to sponsors' products and services is unsurpassed."

"Just because the gross has increased doesn't mean your fans are responsible for it. Other people buy our products, too, you know."

No kidding. "Dad would never have pulled the rug out from under me this way," she said evenly.

"He should never have put it under you to begin with, Gabby. He was always indulgent where you were concerned. Maybe if he hadn't been so sick the last couple of years he would have been able to think more clearly and he would have realized he wasn't doing you any favors."

"There was nothing wrong with Dad's reasoning."

"You saw only one side of Brock, Gabriella. The side you wanted to see. I, on the other hand—"

"Saw a cripple. Yeah, you told me."

Stay calm, Gabby told herself. Don't let her get to you, because she'll use it against you later to prove you're nothing but a self-indulgent, spoiled, ungrateful…

Twenty minutes later Gabby left her mother's office as mad or madder than she'd been when she entered. For her mother to attack Brock was unconscionable. Gabby had loved her father and he had loved her. He would never have done anything to harm her. To imply that he would, that he was incompetent because of his illness was, in Gabby's mind, unforgivable.

She left her mother's office, but she didn't leave the building.

DESMOND FAIRCHILD had been a contemporary of Gabby's father and his best friend since they'd been fraternity brothers at Duke. Gabby no longer called him "Uncle Desmond," the way she had when she was a kid, but the sentiment was still there. Fifty-five years old, with thinning silver hair and a square jaw, he greeted Gabby with a warm embrace and a look of understanding concern.

"Why didn't you tell me what was going on, Des? Did you know she was going to do this?"

"I found out about it only this morning, myself. Magda and I just got back from Europe two days ago."

"How is she?" His wife painted in oils, mostly wildflowers and landscapes from the places they'd traveled.

"Doing great, and she's going to be mad as hell at me if I don't bring you home for dinner soon."

Gabby grinned. Magda was a notoriously bad cook. "How about you let me take you two out to eat instead."

He laughed. "She'll be relieved that she doesn't have to take those pot pies she bought last year out of the freezer. You are talking about the crab place, aren't you?"

It was their favorite restaurant. Gabby laughed. "You're on. I'll check my schedule and call Magda."

They'd wandered over to the conversation pit that occupied a corner of his spacious office. One of Magda's large forest canvases filled the wall behind the couch. Desmond sat beneath it, while Gabby took the love seat at an angle to him.

"So what's going on, Des?" she asked. "I finally got around to reading the fiscal reports you all insist on sending me, and even I can figure out that the bottom line isn't what it was when Dad was CEO. Mom says the decreased profits are because we're spending too much on advertising in the wrong place, namely NASCAR."

He worked his lips.

"You don't agree?"

He shook his head. "I don't think the problem is promotions or advertising. Your dad did very well spending equal amounts, sometimes more, in comparable dollars. But he was the bold and adventurous type. Never met a challenge he wasn't willing to tackle, and he did so till the very end." He took a breath. "Your mother is much more…cautious. Take product expansion. OI made its name by producing high-quality, high-priced products that are classic in design and made to last. But Brock was also looking into expanding into a more utilitarian line of home furnishings. No decision had been made by the time of his death, so it was left to your mother to decide."

"And she nixed it."

Desmond nodded. "She didn't want the O'Farrell name to be diluted by what she called inferior products."

"Did you agree with her?"

"Yes and no. The O'Farrell trademark should always be synonymous with high quality, but that doesn't mean we can't open another line, a subdivision of OI, using a completely different brand name. I'm not suggesting cheap junk, but every piece of furniture doesn't have to be a family heirloom. Computer desks don't have to last a lifetime, for example. The computers sure don't. Neither does their configuration. We have to be flexible."

Gabby could imagine her mother's obstinacy on the issue. "What else?"

"The new plant. We need to expand, modernize, whether we diversify or not. Our sales have been going up but not nearly as fast as they could because we simply don't have the capacity to produce more, and per capita costs have been rising. Della insists on clinging to this nostalgic notion that the old ways are superior to the new, ignoring the fact that technological innovations can also improve quality. Instead of envisioning the increased revenue and profits a more modern, more efficient plant would create, she sees only the cost of construction and the demands of having to meet a larger payroll."

Desmond gave Gabby more examples of Della's refusal to take bold initiatives.

"How does the rest of the board feel about her canceling the NASCAR sponsorship?" she finally asked.

"It's a mixed bag. Leland and Stanley have never been keen on it, feel it's targeting the wrong market. The others are ambivalent or followers."

"Do you think they can be persuaded to change their minds?"

CHAPTER TWENTY-ONE

THE MONDAY MORNING after the race at Pocono, Gabby received a call from Trey David.

"Congratulations on your showing yesterday. Tough race."

She hadn't matched her previous first place in Alabama, but she had come in third, behind Jem Nordstrom and Freddie Harris.

"Were you there?" she asked excitedly. "Why didn't you let me know?"

"Actually, I was in Cleveland on business, but I caught as much of it on TV as I could. You're racking up the points, friend of mine."

She felt that tingle of satisfaction. "Thanks."

"I was wondering if you might be available for dinner with me tomorrow night. Short notice, I know, and if you can't, I certainly understand."

She was supposed to have dinner with Vaughn and Stephanie tonight and Wednesday, but Tuesday was open because her last guest appearance in the afternoon was in Spartanburg, so she wouldn't be able to get back to Greensboro until after Stephanie's suppertime. Grace was very insistent that she keep a regular meal schedule. Considering all the girl had been through, Gabby agreed that maintaining structure in her life was important.

"I'll be in South Carolina all day and don't expect to get home until around eight."

"That's fine," he said. "In fact it works out better for me. Grab yourself a late-afternoon snack and I'll pick you up at your place at nine."

HE WAS PUNCTUAL to the minute, dressed in a Western-cut, light blue sports jacket and open-necked, cream-colored silk shirt. She kept forgetting how tall and incredibly handsome the guy was.

He drove her to a small restaurant behind a strip mall on the other side of town. A bottle of her favorite white wine was already chilling in an ice bucket at the table to which they were led by the tuxedoed maître d' who greeted Trey by name.

"I never even realized this place was here," Gabby commented after they were seated. Starched white linen, hotel silver service, crystal glassware.

"I found it last year. Great food, impeccable service, quiet atmosphere. Nobody will bother us here."

The evening turned out to be more a counseling session than a tryst. Trey was having "woman" problems and wanted her advice. Gabby wasn't sure if she should be complimented or insulted.

He'd mentioned on their drive to his parents' house for their "setup" dinner that he was involved with someone but that he wasn't ready to introduce her to his parents yet. Now he explained in more detail.

Even before he'd taken the newly established post as VP for promotions, he'd helped his father establish a charitable foundation. For the initial presentations of grants he'd gone to recipient institutions personally to meet people and hand over checks.

One of the beneficiaries was a drug rehab center at a retreat in the mountains, and it was there that he'd met Bliss. She was a counselor, two years older than he and divorced from an abusive husband who was currently serving time in prison for aggravated assault and robbery. She had also gained custody of her crackhead sister's two-year-old daughter.

"Sounds like quite a clan," Gabby observed. And not the type that people wanted grafted onto their family tree.

"The whole family's dysfunctional," Trey admitted. "Except Bliss. She's had her problems, too, spent some time in jail for petty theft when she was still a teenager, but in her case it was a wake-up call. She's turned her life around since then."

"And now you want to marry her," Gabby concluded.

"Am I crazy? She's great, and the baby is really growing. Bliss would like to stay home with Chantelle full-time. I've told her when we get married she can, but she's still terrified of meeting my parents, so we have some things to work out yet. But that's not the only reason I wanted to see you."

She raised an eyebrow.

"I hear your mother's pulling the plug on your NASCAR sponsorship," he commented after the waiter had taken their orders.

"She's trying to."

"How can you stop her?"

She mimicked a heavy accent. "I haf my vays."

"Maybe I can help."

"Oh?"

"Interested?"

"I'm all ears."

GRACE WAS STUNNED when at midday on Wednesday she received a telephone call from Della O'Farrell. The two women had hit it off in Atlanta and promised to keep in touch, but Grace hadn't really expected they would. A middle-class homemaker and a Philadelphia mainline corporate exec didn't really have much in common, except as mothers of daughters.

"Have you seen *The Chatterer* this morning?" Della asked excitedly.

A gossip tabloid? "Uh, no. I don't usually—"

Della laughed. "I don't, either, Grace, but I have a clipping service that keeps me posted on anything that has to do with business or family. They're on the front page."

"They? Who?"

"Gabby and Trey David. You know, of *the* Davids. They own Emporico."

Grace certainly knew Emporico. She shopped there regularly. "Who's Trey?"

"Reginald David the Third, son of the founder and CEO. A few months ago I introduced them…Gabby and Trey, I mean. Actually they'd met before, but that was years and years ago, when they were still kids. I was hoping they'd develop an interest in each other. He's a bachelor, handsome as sin and…well, the family has enough money to underwrite the national debt."

"But why are they on the front page of *The Chatterer?*"

All the rag dealt in, as far as Grace could figure from seeing them on display at the checkout line in the supermarket, was scandal and sensationalism. She couldn't understand why Della would sound so pleased to have her daughter's face plastered on the front page.

"Some fan with one of those camera cell phones

found out somehow they were at this very exclusive restaurant in Greensboro Tuesday night and got a picture of them as they were leaving around midnight. They're holding hands and laughing like a couple of teenagers. I asked Gabby a few times if she and Trey were seeing each other. She was always very evasive. Just like her to want to keep it secret that they're getting serious about each other."

Did that mean Grace had been misreading the relationship between Vaughn and Gabby? Could it really have been nothing more than professional friendship and acts of kindness toward Stephanie? She still didn't think so, but…

"I knew I was doing the right thing when I canceled our sponsorship of that silly stock car." Della practically babbled on. "I bet as soon as he got my letter your son-in-law broke off with Gabriella. Any day now she'll come to thank me and announce that she and Trey want to get married. Isn't that wonderful?"

Grace's heart rose. "It sure is." *And I can't wait to tell Vaughn all about it.*

TO VAUGHN it didn't make any sense. Yeah, he'd seen *The Chatterer*'s front-page photo even before Grace had called to tell him about it. One of his PR people had dropped it on his desk that morning. Gabby and this guy, Trey David, holding hands and laughing. She looked happy, gleeful, and pretty boy… He looked like he was having a good time, too. Too good.

It wasn't jealousy, Vaughn told himself. Gabby had the right to go to dinner with any-damn-one she pleased. He was just concerned about her getting that kind of publicity.

Being "exposed" in *The Chatterer* wasn't something you listed in your credits.

Okay, so the caption and short article that accompanied the picture—obviously a candid shot—were positive. This time. But even when a write-up in that rag was complimentary, the impression was tawdry. That wasn't how Vaughn or NASCAR wanted his team to be perceived.

Did this mean that with her sponsorship cut off Gabby had decided it was time to end her racing career, marry some rich guy and settle down to raise two point three kids?

He remembered her reputation for getting excited about doing things, then just as quickly dropping them for the next challenge.

She'd never said anything about this David character, never even mentioned his name. Vaughn began to wonder if she'd been playing with him, if he'd been just a convenient diversion.

They'd made love—several times. Didn't that mean anything to her? Could she be sleeping with two men at the same time?

CHAPTER TWENTY-TWO

DELLA WAS NOT ONE to pace, but she did that morning. Up and down the length of the Aubusson carpet in her office. Across it. Diagonally.

The just-concluded discussion she'd had with Desmond Fairchild had her steaming. The board had the gall to demand a revisit of her decision to drop OI's sponsorship of Gabby in NASCAR. Challenging her on a decision she'd already made and that they'd rubber-stamped was bad enough, but when Della realized that Gabby had been lobbying against her behind her back... Well, that was far worse.

She and Gabby had had their disagreements over the years, but then she supposed all mothers and daughters did. She'd certainly had her share with her own mother, though with the insight of maturity and experience Della had to admit Leticia Meriwether-Colbert had often been right. But for Gabby to question Della's authority as CEO of O'Farrell Industries was simply intolerable.

Returning to her desk, Della conferred the schedule her secretary had been able to obtain from Vaughn Steiner's PR department. Gabby was in Wilmington today speaking at some school. Didn't really matter. She'd have her cell phone with her.

She was about to hit the speed dial when she had a second

thought. She'd deal with Gabby later. First she had to settle another score. She pressed the button to her intercom.

"Bonnie, find out where Vaughn Steiner is today."

Ten minutes later she was told he was at his garage in Charlotte, was expected to be there all day, but would be leaving first thing in the morning for the Brickyard, whatever that was.

"Notify him I'll be there in two hours. Also call the airport and tell Sergio to file a flight plan for Charlotte. Let him know I'm leaving here now and want to take off when I get there. Also, have Keenan bring the car around, and since I'm not sure when I'll be back, cancel all my appointments for the rest of the day."

An hour later the Learjet was taxiing on the private side of Charlotte-Douglas Airport. She'd ordered not just a car but a stretch limo to be waiting for her when she landed. Under ideal conditions she would have ordered Steiner to come to her, but she didn't want to wait, and since that meant she was forced to appear on his territory, she might as well do it in a power vehicle.

She smiled when she was waived through the gate at the Steiner Racing compound. In Steiner's place she would have had him wait long enough to make the point that she was a guest on his turf, that she was in control. People thought the source of power was money, but they were wrong. Real power derived from psychology and will. All great leaders knew that.

He was standing outside the doorway under the steel canopy to the three-story stucco building when her car slowed to a stop. Another missed opportunity on his part, she noted. He should have had her taken to him, rather than been waiting obeisance on her. Clearly he wasn't into what he probably thought of as playing games. Fine. She would say what she had to say and leave. The chauffeur opened her door for her.

"Della." Steiner extended his left hand to assist her.

She ignored it. His tone was upbeat, welcoming, she noted. The fool probably thought with all the positive publicity her daughter was getting lately, she was here to negotiate a new sponsorship program.

"How nice to see you," he said. "Have you come for a tour of our facilities?"

"Mr. Steiner," she replied formally, putting an instant chill in the air, "is there someplace we can talk privately?"

His face remained immobile, but she could see the uneasiness, the questions in his brown eyes.

"Of course."

He motioned for her to precede him into the building. The automatic doors soughed open.

The lobby was an almost perfect cube of space. Several stock cars were on display, each with the number 111, presumably the cars he'd driven. Della hadn't realized Gabby was using *his* number. Several banners and flags hung from the ceiling. The walls were festooned with posters. Glass cases were crammed with trophies and other memorabilia from the track.

Vaughn led her to the left, to a set of double glass doors that opened to a long corridor. On the right was a series of doors. On the left, a waist-to-ceiling wall of windows looked out on a garage.

The first thing that struck Della was how clean everything was. In her mind garages were dirty, grimy places where you had to watch your step and touching anything was at your peril. This work center was spotless, the floor painted glossy gray. If there were any oil spills they were well-hidden. Mechanics were working on vehicles that appeared to be in various stages of assembly, and they were wearing jumpsuits that were clean and neat and, of all things, white.

At the far end of the hallway they came to another set of double doors, these paneled mahogany. Vaughn opened the right one, stepped through and stood aside for her to follow. The woman behind the reception desk, probably not much younger than Della, rose in place.

"May I bring you something to drink?" she asked.

Vaughn deferred to Della, who declined.

They went into the inner office. He motioned her into a chair in front of his desk. Like everything else she'd seen, the room was clean and orderly.

"Mrs. O'Farrell," he said, matching her previous formal tone, "what can I do for you?"

"I want to make clear, Mr. Steiner, just so there won't be any misunderstandings, that O'Farrell Industries will not be sponsoring my daughter in NASCAR."

"So you said in the letter you sent me. I'm sorry you don't think the investment is worthwhile, and I know Gabby is very disappointed. She's done well, Mrs. O'Farrell, especially since this is her first season, and has a very promising career ahead of her. She'll do you and your company proud, if you'll give her a chance."

"My decision is a sound one, Mr. Steiner, based on proven business principles. Whether you or she agree with it doesn't justify her trying to undermine me."

"Undermine you?" He cocked his head to one side. "I'm afraid you have me at a disadvantage, Mrs. O'Farrell. I have no idea what you're talking about."

"Don't you?" But the expression on his face, the confusion reflected in those beguiling brown eyes—no wonder Gabby was under his spell—indicated to her that he was telling the truth. Gabby had done things behind her back, why should Della be surprised that she had done things behind his, as well.

Either that or he was a damn good actor.

"My daughter has been conspiring with members of the OI board of directors to question my decision to drop our sponsorship of your racing team. Are you telling me you know nothing about it?"

"Conspiring? That's a pretty strong word."

"So you're not denying awareness of what she's doing."

She could see his first impulse was to challenge her statement, but he didn't, which was a little disappointing. Instead he allowed his hands to hang from the ends of the padded armrests and stared at her intently for several very long seconds.

"Somehow I don't think it will make any difference to you whether I denied it or not, but just for the record I have no knowledge of any dealings Gabby has had with anyone at OI, including you."

He kept his voice low, so low that she had to concentrate on what he was saying. She was used to men raising their voices when they were impassioned about something. It was their clumsy way of showing strength, dominance. When she was young the shouting of men like her father frightened her. In more recent years she'd found it more annoying than intimidating, but there was something menacing in the way Vaughn Steiner practically whispered his comments. To the point that she found herself squirming in her seat.

"Let me remind you, Mr. Steiner, that I am the CEO and president of OI, which gives me considerable unilateral decision-making authority. The board may have the legal right to ask me to reconsider an executive decision, but I promise you that I will fight—in court if need be—any attempt on their part to undermine that authority. My husband worked his entire life to make OI what it is. I take my responsibility to continue that work very seriously. I'm not about to see it destroyed by one of Gabriella's flights of fancy."

Della settled a little deeper into the upholstered chair, more confident of her command of the situation now. Steiner hadn't made a move since she started, hadn't raised an objection or mounted a defense of himself or Gabby. She took that as a good sign. He obviously realized his cause was lost.

"Don't be misled by my daughter's little acts of rebellion, Mr. Steiner. She loved her father very much and won't do anything to tarnish his memory. When all this foolishness is over she'll be as committed to OI as I am. She's amused herself with this racing business longer than she has with any of her other diversions, but now that she's proved herself by winning a race, she has no reason to continue. I've been tolerant and patient with her, but my indulgence is at an end. It's time she returned to her rightful place in society."

He sat there in silence, unmoved. She found herself compelled to fill the void.

"Gabriella will be announcing her engagement to Reginald David the Third very soon now. You can be sure Trey isn't going to allow his wife to continue to race cars."

Did she see a flicker of something in Steiner's eyes when she mentioned Gabby's involvement with the son of one of the wealthiest men in the country? Still, he said nothing. Her husband used to do that, too, fight her with a wall of silence. It was nerve-racking.

"Which brings me to my final point, Mr. Steiner. If you care about my daughter, at all, you'll sever your personal relationship with her immediately. Not only will it harm her reputation if it becomes public, but it has the potential to do serious damage to your career, as well. I understand NASCAR takes a very dim view of sex scandals."

She rose. He did the same, though more slowly. She stood, ladylike, waiting for him to come around the side of the desk. He walked casually to the door, opened it and let her pass through.

He didn't say a word as he accompanied her to her waiting limousine.

It wasn't until she'd started to get into it that he finally spoke up. "Do you know what a dagger is, Mrs. O'Farrell?"

Catching her bent over in a rather undignified posture, she stared back at him.

"It's a double-edged knife used for stabbing," he said. "Be very careful you don't cut yourself with it."

She glared at him, speechless and confused, then hurried to settle onto the luxury car's soft leather upholstery. Had he just threatened her? She wasn't sure. What exactly did he mean? She didn't know. What she did know was that his words, spoken so softly, so calmly, held a foreboding quality that frightened her.

CHAPTER TWENTY-THREE

GABBY PULLED UP in front of Steiner Racing in her bright red Mustang convertible a little after two o'clock Thursday afternoon, greeted Millie at the reception desk, got the all-clear and after a discrete knock, practically danced into the office.

"Hi," she said, standing just inside the doorway.

She was feeling keyed-up and excited inside. This weekend was the race in Indianapolis, the most prestigious and heavily attended NASCAR race of the season. Three hundred thousand people would fill the stands and millions more would be watching it live on TV. Naturally, Gabby was looking forward to it.

Vaughn was at his desk, a pencil in his right hand, intent over papers.

"You look awfully industrious," she said. He looked up at her, and she saw the sullen expression on his face. "Is something wrong?"

"Close the door."

"Uh-oh," she said, only half in jest. She did as she was told and approached the desk. "Sounds serious."

"Your mother came to see me this morning."

"Mom? Here?" Like a balloon that was deflating, she collapsed into the chair Della had previously occupied. "Why?"

"To reiterate what she said in her letter, that OI isn't going to sponsor you anymore."

"She came all this way just to tell you that?"

"She told me you've been conspiring behind her back to get the board to overturn her decision."

"Conspiracy, huh?" Gabby was tempted to smile, but the somber cast of his eyes dissuaded her. "If she'd had the guts to talk to me face to face, I would have told her up front what I was planning to do. As it is, I believe I have enough votes to override her decision."

"She's threatening to go to court and fight any attempt to challenge her authority."

"That's ridiculous." But Gabby could feel her stomach muscles clench. She hated these battles with her mother.

"Maybe, but that's the way things stand."

Gabby realized she shouldn't be completely surprised at this move by her mother. It was typical of her. She knew she couldn't win in a one-on-one confrontation with Gabby, so she was circling around, using her formidable capacity to intimidate someone who wasn't as familiar with her weak spots.

Oh, Della was good at making threats, whether she intended to carry them out or not, calculating that the seriousness of the threat would be enough for her to get her way. It hadn't worked in years, not since Gabby was a teenager. She'd wanted to act in a play at school that her mother didn't approve of. Anything less than Shakespeare was unworthy, according to Della. She'd threatened to take away Gabby's new BMW, if she persisted. Gabby had called her bluff and taken the lead role in the slapstick comedy anyway. She knew her mother wouldn't take away the sporty little coupe convertible. It simply wouldn't have looked right for the daughter of Brock and Della O'Farrell to not have a car, and of course if she was going to have a car it had to be a socially significant one, not some old clunker. Since then, Gabby had blown off most of her threats.

"Look, Gabby," Vaughn said, "I don't know anything about what you've been doing behind the scenes—"

"Did you tell her that?"

"I tried to but she made it very clear she wasn't interested in anything I had to say."

"Yeah, that's Mom," Gabby said with a sigh.

"The point is, I'm in an untenable situation here. Maybe you have the legal power to force her hand. I don't know anything about that. The problem is we can't afford a public scandal. It won't do OI any good and could hurt your business, even put it in jeopardy if what she says is true, that OI can't afford the cost of sponsorship. NASCAR doesn't look favorably on getting in the middle of family feuds. It's a no-win situation."

"OI's committed for this season," she said, unable to keep from raising her voice. "Mom can't renege on it without violating the agreement Dad made, the very same contract she signed a few months ago, not without landing in court, herself. She's not about to let that happen, Vaughn, first because it would be very bad for public relations. Second because breaking a commitment of this size without due cause—and she doesn't have any—would destroy OI's reputation and adversely impact its stock. And third, because those two factors together would get her booted as CEO. I'm not the only one pissed off at what she's doing. Trust me, Vaughn, my mother thrives on her position and title as president and chief executive officer and all the perks and prestige they garner. She'd not going to jeopardize them. As for a family feud—" Gabby scoffed "—not a chance. Della abhors scandal. The sanctity of the O'Farrell name is sacred to her. She's not going to do anything that will leave it open to ridicule."

Vaughn just sat there studying her. Surely, he didn't doubt she was right. It was so obvious Della was a vain woman and a vindictive one, as well.

"Your mother also said you and this guy Trey David are getting ready to—"

"Trey? Oh, don't worry about him." She snorted with dismissive amusement. "My mother set me up with him a few months back and has probably convinced herself we're going to get married and raise a mansion full of kids. Forget Trey. Just think of him as a friend, that's all."

"Well, I'm relieved to hear there won't be any scandal," he said after what seemed like a long pause. "No one comes out a winner in a situation like that except the media."

Vaughn pushed back in his chair. "Under the circumstances, Gabby, I think it would be prudent for us to cool it for a while."

"Cool it? You mean—"

"Not see each other off the track. We've been lucky so far to keep our…friendship out of the public eye, but it's only a matter of time. Let's quit while we're ahead."

What the hell was that supposed to mean?

"Also, in light of your mother's obvious dislike of me, I suggest that if you intend to continue to race in NASCAR, that you start looking for another team for next year. Maybe with someone else in charge, your mother will reconsider granting you a sponsorship."

Gabby sat there, staring at him, devastated. She loved racing. It had taken her twenty-two years to discover what was in her blood, and it was racing. Now she was hearing that her career might be over.

More than racing, though, she'd come to love Vaughn, and she thought he loved her. Had the days and evenings they spent together, alone and with Stephanie, been nothing more than a pleasant pastime for him? Had the nights they'd shared meant nothing more to him than a release of sexual tension?

Her father had taught her to fight for what she really wanted, and what she really wanted was to race. She wasn't going to give that up. There wasn't any substitute for the exhilaration of racing. Nothing.

CHAPTER TWENTY-FOUR

"SO THAT'S IT?" She exploded. "My mother throws a tizzy-fit about me racing in NASCAR, and you just toss me overboard?"

"I'm not tossing you overboard, Gabby," he said. "It's just that—"

"The hell you aren't. Her threats are hollow, Vaughn. I know my mother. In spite of all the bravado and posturing, she's weak. Call her bluff. Stand up to her and she'll crumple. I guarantee it."

Gabby got up and started pacing. "You're worried about NASCAR frowning on a family feud. I assure you my mother is far more sensitive about losing face with her society friends. A public spectacle of rebellion within her precious corporation would be devastating and humiliating. She'll back down at the slightest hint of that actually happening."

Gabby stood behind her chair and looked directly at him. "That's where I have the advantage over her. I don't give a damn what people think, so they don't hold power over me. But what people think is vitally important to Della O'Farrell. Call her bluff," she repeated, begged. "Tell her you'll sue if she doesn't honor the company's pledge to sponsor me."

"You said she'll honor this year's commitment," he reminded her. "What would be the point of threatening legal action for something she'll already do?"

"The contract was for two years, enough time, my father figured, to find out if I had what it takes."

"But each year is independent," Vaughn pointed out. "It's essentially a one-year contract with an option for a second."

"With a *commitment* for a second," she corrected him, "unless circumstances intervened, like me not being able or willing to drive for some reason, or if my performance was so poor that you were withdrawing me from competition. That hardly seems justified when I'm headed for the Chase for the NASCAR NEXTEL Cup."

"I understand all that," Vaughn said, "and I've discussed it with our lawyers. They vetted the contract very carefully, but it turns out there's wiggle room that your mother can use to say that OI also has the option of withdrawing their sponsorship, if in their opinion, it's not an economically productive relationship."

"They can't prove that. Sales are up. It's profits that are down, and I'm willing to bet if we did a survey we'd find that NASCAR fans are responsible for the increased gross."

"That's all well and good," Vaughn replied, "and we might even win the argument in a court of law. The problem is that it would take time and money to prove our point. By then we'd both be losers."

He just didn't understand.

Gabby blew out a breath in frustration. "Okay, let me spell it out for you. Go back to Della and remind her of the option clause. Tell her that unless she picks it up for next year you'll announce to the media that she has refused to support her own daughter in her race for the Cup."

He started to object.

She ignored him and rushed on. "In spite of the fact that I've been racking up points and have an excellent chance of being the first woman in NASCAR history to win the Cup."

"Gabby, that's blackmail."

"Arm-twisting maybe. But it's all part of the game of duck-and-weave in the corporate world."

"I won't use tactics like that to get sponsor support. Aside from the fact that it's unethical, it would be stupid. Once word got out about my arm-twisting, as you call it, no one would ever want to sponsor a team of mine for fear of being put in the same vulnerable position."

"No one will ever find out about it because we're not going to tell them and Della sure as hell isn't about to disclose to anyone that she was outmaneuvered."

"I won't do it."

She sighed. "No, I didn't think you would, but it was worth a try. Maybe I'll do it myself."

"Gabby, don't." There was a plea in his voice. "You'll lose something more valuable than a few million dollars."

He was right, of course, and that only incensed her more. "So we're back to you dumping me."

He shook his head, a look of frustration on his face. "I'm not dumping you, Gabby. We still have the rest of this season."

"Then I'm on my own. The first sign of opposition and you tell me to get lost, find myself another sponsor, as well as another team to race for. You don't call that abandonment?"

"With your record for this rookie season, you won't have any problem finding a sponsor, if you really want to go on racing."

She spun around, her brows raised. "Oh, so that's it. My mother has convinced you this is just a passing fancy, that it was fun as long as I had my daddy's money to finance it, but now with that gone I'll move on to other things. I suppose my mother also has you convinced I need to take my rightful, ladylike place on the board of OI, marry some rich millionaire and raise a slew of kids for her to spoil."

He averted his eyes, looked as if he were about to say something. When he didn't, she lashed out.

"I would have thought after what we've experienced together, Vaughn, that you would know me better than that. I guess I was confusing lust with affection, narrow-mindedness with determination."

"Are you finished?" His words were clipped, angry.

"Almost." She stomped across the carpet and back again, came to a halt behind her chair and braced her hands on its back. "I stood by you when skeptics were questioning whether you had the business acumen to organize and lead a winning team. I defended you when your critics were speculating that you were hooked on prescribed medications. I had faith in you, Vaughn."

She strode to the door, put her hand on the knob. With her back still to him, her voice bounced off the mahogany panel. "Too bad you don't have the same faith in me."

"I—"

But she was gone.

SHE WAITED UNTIL she was in her motor coach before she gave in to the emotions cascading through her.

Anger at her mother, but that wasn't anything new. She could handle Della. She was more upset with herself for not anticipating the woman's move.

Her real fury was directed at Vaughn. These past months had been heady, to say the least. She was doing what she most wanted to do, and she was doing it well. Even more, she'd found a man she'd fallen in love with.

Now she felt forsaken.

As she leaned forward, her hands braced against the edge of the marble kitchen counter, she let the tears that had been building tumble to the floor. Her whole body shuddered as the pain of his abandonment built inside her.

What seemed like ages later she grabbed a couple of tissues from the dispenser by the telephone and dried her eyes. Then she went to the refrigerator and got out a bottle of spring water, raspberry flavored, and let its tang cool the hot lump in the back of her throat. She went over to the couch and lay on the butter-soft leather. Time to think. Enough self-pity. Enough dwelling on the negative. It was time to decide what to do next. Patently obvious was that she couldn't count on other people. She'd have to take full control of the situation and herself.

After several minutes, she got up, found her cell phone and hit a number.

"Hi, Trey. I just want to make sure we're still on for tonight."

CHAPTER TWENTY-FIVE

HIS SHOWDOWN with Gabby wasn't a good start to one of the most important weekends of the season, so Vaughn was surprised when things went well, though he kept waiting for the other shoe to fall.

Indianapolis was the granddaddy of auto race tracks. Almost a century old, it was the longest continuously operating track in the world. The two-and-a-half-mile course was also one of the most daunting challenges, especially to the uninitiated.

Technically an oval because the corners were rounded rather than squared, it was actually rectangular in shape with four ninety-degree turns separated by four straightaways, and unlike tracks designed for stock cars, those straightaways were flat, not banked. That meant that while high speeds could be achieved, a good deal of braking was required to negotiate the unusually tight turns. For spectators facing the end of a long leg, the sight of cars screaming directly at them at top speed could be terrifying…and exciting.

Maybe it was determination born of anger that made Gabby hyperalert and super-aggressive on the Indy track. Or maybe it was her resolve to "show him." Whatever the reason, she took the pole position in the qualification laps on Friday afternoon, the first NASCAR rookie to ever do so at that track and, of course, the first woman to achieve that distinction.

On Sunday she held the lead for three laps but stability problems forced her to pull into the pits twice to have wedges installed, first in the rear, then in the front. As a result she lost the lead, but not for long. After a hundred and fifty laps she was back in first place. Ten laps later she took the checkered flag.

The adrenaline of victory was everywhere. She was ecstatic. Her crew chief and team patted themselves on the backs. Stephanie bounced up and down and yelled her head off. Naturally the car owner was proud, too. Genuinely proud. His team was showing its mettle, especially since Brett came in fifth, in spite of a blown tire on the fortieth lap.

Winning was what NASCAR racing was all about, and Gabby O'Farrell was clearly on her way to becoming a strong contender for the NASCAR NEXTEL Cup, if not this year, then next year or the year after that. Provided she stayed in the race.

Would she?

She said she would, that NASCAR was her life.

Her mother said otherwise, that Gabby was a dilettante, that she played with professions and lifestyles until she was tired of them, then dropped them like old news. Did that apply to people, as well?

The heart of the problem, though, wasn't whether Gabby could win the race or whether she would stay the course. The problem was that he'd trusted her. He'd thought their "relationship," as Della called it, meant something more to her than a convenient diversion. Yet all the time she'd been seeing another man. If her friendship with Trey David was so innocent, why hadn't she ever mentioned him? She'd made light of the notion that she might marry this guy and settle down to raise a family, but she'd never actually denied it.

When exactly had she planned to tell him? Before she made the public announcement? Or was she just going to let him read about it in the papers?

He felt like a fool. A simpleminded nincompoop.

He had no experience with women who used sex as a plaything, as a form of amusement, entertainment. Call him gullible. Call him unsophisticated. Call him stupid. He'd trusted her, projected his own feelings onto her, made the incredibly naive mistake of assuming she felt the same way about him as he felt about her.

Invited to the party later that evening at the local watering hole, he made an appearance, shook hands and thanked everyone for their support and bought a round of drinks to add to the festivities, but he didn't linger. The adult party wasn't appropriate for children and he reminded everyone he needed to get back to his young daughter. They were planning to fly home that evening, so he needed to get started.

No one questioned his bugging out. Instead they sent their regards to the little girl everyone had adopted as a sort of mascot. Gabby had already said goodbye to Grace and given Stephanie a great big hug before coming over to the bar. Now she was out on the dance floor with Brett. Vaughn left without saying goodbye to her.

Stephanie was outside playing with Cindy and her growing pup when he got back to the coach. Grandma, she told him, was inside finishing with the packing.

He mounted the steps and opened the door.

He could hear Grace in the bedroom talking to someone, and from the volume of her speech he knew immediately she must be on her cell phone. It was an old joke that she spoke louder when she was on her cell.

"They can barely stand being around each other," Grace was saying with obvious satisfaction. "At least in private. No more lovey-dovey… Oh, they put on a good front in public, polite, even joke around. Someone who didn't know any better probably wouldn't notice anything was wrong. But they can't fool me… Yeah, she did very well today, Della. From what I heard nobody expected her to even make the top ten and she managed to come in first. The media was all over her… Yes, we're flying back tonight, which is fine by me… I'll be glad when this season's over… Della, he'll be back in a few minutes and I still have to finish packing… Yes, I'll talk to you later in the week and let you know how things are going… I'm relieved, too."

Vaughn was leaning against the kitchen island, his arms folded across his chest, when Grace emerged from the bedroom not ten seconds later, probably to retrieve the can of soda she'd left sitting on the counter next to the refrigerator. She stopped dead in her tracks when she saw him, her eyes went wide and her jaw perceptibly dropped.

"Oh," she muttered a second later. "I didn't hear you come in."

"No, I don't suppose you did." He stared at her and let the moment linger. Finally he said, "I'll be outside with Steph. Let me know when you're ready. I know you're anxious to get home."

"Vaughn," she called out in panic as he turned the handle of the door.

"Yes?" he said over his shoulder.

"Nothing. It'll only take me a couple of minutes."

Without responding, he stepped outside.

SOMEHOW HE AND GRACE managed to keep the tension between them below Stephanie's radar on the short drive out to the Learjet. The six-year-old kept prattling on about Gabby, how everyone was talking about her winning the race and that she was going to make the cut for the Chase for the NASCAR NEXTEL Cup.

At least he didn't have to fake his confidence or his enthusiasm that she did indeed have a very good chance.

Once airborne, Stephanie dozed, Grace knitted while she watched a movie on DVD and he sipped a tall Scotch and soda, a rare indulgence for him. Why had he never realized how negative Grace was toward Gabby or about NASCAR? He'd seen her early reserve about Gabby, the small flutter of what might have been jealousy. He'd shrugged it off as the normal reaction of a woman protecting her family from outsiders. But overhearing her conversation with Della told him this was more than that, and he was having a hard time making sense out of it.

At some point he and Grace were going to have to discuss it, but not yet. First he had to get past the raw feeling of having been betrayed by two women he'd trusted. He'd also have to wait until Stephanie wasn't around. He sincerely hoped he and his mother-in-law could resolve the situation. He appreciated all she'd done, respected her for it and needed her.

He realized sadly, however, that he could dismiss Grace from his life easily enough, that despite the two years of living under the same roof, they weren't close. Still, Grace was important to his daughter. Stephanie needed the continuity and security of having her grandmother around, so for her sake he'd try his best to mend the rift between them, come to some sort of truce and alliance, at least until Stephanie was older and could make her own decisions about how involved she wanted her grandma to be in her life.

As for Grace's dislike of Gabby, was it because she was a NASCAR driver and, like Della, Grace considered the profession too dangerous and inappropriate for a woman? Was it because Gabby was tempting Stephanie in the same direction? Vaughn wasn't fooling himself. Steph's fascination with driving could wane as quickly as it had waxed.

Or was Grace's hostility more generic, visceral? Would she oppose any woman who might threaten to replace Lisa? He should have considered the possibility sooner, but he'd been blinded by his own feelings, by the hope rushing through him, to consider the effects on others of his infatuation.

After Lisa died, until he met Gabby, he'd been reconciled to a celibate life, and now perhaps he would have to reconcile himself to it again. Unless he found that special woman who could fill the void inside him. He thought he'd found it in Gabby, and God knew, he still ached for her.

He needed to get away. To think.

"HEY, STEPH," Vaughn said as he tucked her into bed later that night, "what say we take a trip tomorrow to Transylvania County and see the waterfalls? I've never seen them and I hear they're spectacular."

"Awesome. Is Gabby coming, too?"

"Afraid not, peanut. She has a bunch of things to do, guest appearances and book signings, so she can't get away. It'll be just the two of us. What do you say?"

"I wish she was coming with us."

"I know, honey."

The idea of Gabby with another man tormented him, but the thought of what her duplicity in their relationship was about to do to his daughter infuriated him. Stephanie had grown close to Gabby, come to look up to her, if not as a mother substitute, something pretty close, a friend she could count on. Now Gabby was about to betray her, too.

"Maybe some other time when she's not so busy, but that may not be for a while. With the end of the racing season coming, her schedule is going to be even more hectic than it's been so far. She'll have a lot of guest appearances and other appointments to keep. We probably shouldn't count on her being around too much."

"I miss her."

He hugged his little girl. "Things will get better. I promise."

He just hoped it was a promise he could keep.

CHAPTER TWENTY-SIX

VAUGHN WAS UP at seven. He normally had coffee with Grace, but this morning she'd left a note saying she was having breakfast with some friends from church, after which they were going shopping in Raleigh. Or was it to have a powwow with Della? She hoped he and Steph had a good time looking at the falls and added a footnote that she'd fixed lunch for them to take along. He'd find it marked in the refrigerator. A peace offering of sorts, or just insurance that her granddaughter got something wholesome to eat?

He woke his daughter at seven-thirty. She dressed by rote rather than design, ate a bowl of cereal and they were on the road a little after eight o'clock.

Steph slept all the way through Winston-Salem, Statesville and Hickory. From there they climbed into the full majesty of towering green mountains. It was almost eleven o'clock when they finally approached Ashville.

"Hungry, kiddo?" She'd had a small bottle of orange juice after waking an hour earlier, so he figured by now she must be starving.

"Can I have a cheeseburger? Grandma always makes me have grilled chicken. But I like cheeseburgers."

"We could stop at a picnic area," he told her. "Grandma

packed a lunch for us." He'd checked it out. "Chicken salad sandwiches and potato salad."

Stephanie screwed up her mouth. "She always puts pecans in the chicken salad and that bread—" whole-grain wheat berry "—is yucky. I like white bread."

"And you like Gabby's potato salad better."

He wished he hadn't mentioned her name, not that she wasn't constantly on his mind.

"I wish she was with us."

"I do, too," he admitted. He missed her. The old Gabby. The one that made him feel good about the world, about himself. Not the calculating manipulator he'd found out about last Thursday.

"She's very busy right now, Steph. It's—"

"Close to the end of the season. Yeah, you told me." The girl's adult sarcasm startled him. Was she more aware of what was going on than he was giving her credit for? "But I still miss her."

They drove on in silence for another couple of minutes.

"So can I have a cheeseburger and fries, Daddy?"

It seemed a shame to waste the food Grace had prepared.

"On one condition," he said. "You don't tell Grandma. She went to a lot of trouble to fix lunch for us. It wouldn't be nice to tell her we didn't eat it."

Stephanie looked over and grinned at him, and for a second he saw the gleam of a much older woman in her eye. "You're on, Daddy," she said, sounding just like Gabby. "I promise not to breathe a word."

Uh-oh, he thought. I may be contributing to the feminine wiles of my own daughter.

He laughed and pulled off the interstate at the next exit for Ashville. Downtown he'd find a variety of restaurants, but the strip leading to it harbored all the usual fast-food places. He pulled into a popular burger joint, had to wait a minute until someone pulled out of a parking space, since it was lunchtime, and locked the car when they got out.

They had cheeseburgers and fries, but he drew a line at the milk shake his precocious daughter wanted to go with it and convinced her to have juice instead.

"Maybe we can stop and have milk shakes later this afternoon."

She gazed at him doubtfully but didn't argue.

A half hour and a shared fried apple pie later—the milk shake seemed like an insignificant victory now—they were back on the road, this time heading south to Hendersonville. From there they took a secondary road to Brevard in the heart of Transylvania County.

"WHAT IS THIS all about?" Della sat opposite Gabby and Desmond Fairchild at the conference table in the boardroom. They'd insisted on meeting her here instead of in her office, and she had no idea why.

"Della, dear," Fairchild said, "we thought it would be easier for you and everyone if we talked about this in private rather than in the presence of the entire board."

She was instantly on alert. "Talk about what? Des, now what's going on?"

Gabby squirmed with impatience but managed to keep her voice low and inoffensive. "Mother, we would like you to resign as CEO of OI."

Della stared at her, blankly at first, then her eyes grew wider as the message sank in. "You what?" Her tone was somewhere between disbelief and outrage.

"We want you to stay on as president of the company, of course," Desmond said, as if it were a foregone conclusion.

"You're not serious. You can't mean this."

Gabby nodded. "You stay on as president, Mother, and Des will take over as CEO, running day-to-day operations."

"I don't understand." She looked at Desmond, Brock's best friend, someone she'd thought was her friend, too. "Why are you doing this?"

"It's strictly a matter of business, my dear," he said. "Nothing personal."

"As you've pointed out," Gabby went on, "OI profits have been declining, even though sales are up. We feel this is a result of poor management, not market forces. You've passed up several opportunities to increase our output and improve our efficiency. We don't feel your decisions have been good for the company."

Della focused the full power of her laser-beam stare on her daughter. "Is this your idea of payback? I refused to continue your sponsorship in NASCAR, so now you're leading a cabal to have me deposed?"

She sprang from her seat, but her legs didn't seem to have the strength to support her. She flopped back down into the thickly padded leather thrown at the head of the table.

"For shame, Gabriella," she said in her most menacing undertone. "For shame."

Gabby was grateful to Des for suggesting they meet on neutral ground. If they were in CEO's office right now, Della would have ordered them out.

The older woman's hands fluttered. Her voice quavered. "Thank God your father isn't here to see this, Gabriella. He'd be heartbroken at the disrespect and ingratitude you're showing. At your treachery."

Gabby had expected this. She'd spent several sleepless nights mulling over the very thought, ever since she and Desmond had first broached the possibility of separating the two offices. Della's role henceforth would be principally ceremonial, but it would allow her to save face.

"I don't think he would, Mother," she answered firmly, "but that's immaterial. Despite what you think, this is not about me. It's about the good of the company. We're prepared to discuss in detail the problems that have developed since you became CEO, but I think you know what they are."

"All this so you can continue to drive stock cars at OI's expense." Della scoffed. "And you're telling me it's not about you? I knew you were selfish, Gabriella. I knew you disliked my decisions, but this...this goes beyond—"

"It's not about my sponsorship in NASCAR," Gabby insisted.

"I don't believe you. It is about NASCAR. You're being selfish and vindictive."

"Believe what you will, Mother. I'm not going to argue the matter with you, but I will point out that this close-mindedness of yours is symptomatic of the problem. You believe what you want, regardless of the reality staring you in the face."

"The reality is that you hate me because I won't sanction your egotistical frivolities."

Gabby closed her eyes and took a deep breath. "I don't hate you, Mother," she said with soft resignation.

"You could have fooled me."

Desmond stepped in. "Gabby isn't asking for OI to reinstate its previous commitment to Steiner Racing, Della. That's not an issue."

"I'll find someone else to sponsor me," Gabby added, just so her mother wouldn't get the idea that she was giving up racing.

"Della, let me reiterate," Desmond said, "that we're not asking for you to resign as president—"

"You'll have plenty of duties and public exposure as—" Gabby started to interject.

"The board will never approve of this…coup," Della stormed. "I'll fight you. I'll take you to court, if I have to."

"Now who's being selfish and egotistical?" Gabby countered. "Here's a news flash, Mother. The board has already approved this request and is prepared to vote you out of office, if you refuse to resign."

Della stiffened. "When? We've had no meeting."

"In a straw vote, Mother. But it's solid. If you force the issue, I guarantee you'll lose."

"So you really have been conspiring behind my back," Della declared with a hint of smug satisfaction that she'd been right.

"I'm not going to play word games with you, Mom. If it salves your conscience to characterize it that way, go right ahead. But I don't remember your calling me to say you were going to persuade the board to drop my NASCAR sponsorship."

"All you had to do was come to the meeting and you would have known."

"You're absolutely right."

No one spoke for a solid minute. The lengthening silence became unnerving, unbearable.

"I know this comes as a shock, Della," Desmond finally said. "I wish we could have handled it differently. Perhaps if I hadn't been out of the country for so long—"

"But you agree with this…rebellion," Della nearly shouted, her sense of hurt and outrage unmistakable.

Since it was as much a statement as a question, he didn't address it. At least, not directly.

"I've taken the liberty of preparing the paperwork," he said in a calm, businesslike manner. "There's a letter of resignation as CEO and a statement for release to the media explaining that you want to devote more time to private pursuits and to promoting the OI image. You don't have to sign it now. Take some time to think it over, confer with your lawyer, if you like and, of course, we can adjust the verbiage if my words don't suit you."

"The next board meeting will be in two weeks," Gabby reminded her. "That'll be a good time to announce the change. If you haven't signed the letter by then, I'll call for a vote and we'll remove you from office. I really don't want to do that, Mother, but I think you know I will, if you force my hand."

Della rose from her chair and this time stayed on her feet. Her eyes were dry and fierce as she glared at her daughter. "You've gone too far this time, Gabriella. I've tolerated your disrespect, your insults. I've put up with your lack of focus and commitment. I've even endured your disdain for the advantages your father and I have given you. But this time you've gone too far."

She walked to the door, her head held high. With her hand on the knob, she turned around. "I'm glad your father isn't here to witness this stab in the back, this dagger—" She stopped abruptly, as if she'd just remembered something. She closed her eyes briefly, then turned and left the room, leaving the door open behind her.

"Well, that went well," Gabby muttered.

Desmond gathered up the unopened folder with the letter of resignation. "I'll put this in a sealed envelope and deliver it to her office." He wrapped his arm around Gabby's shoulder. "She's upset. Give her a couple of days to calm down. She'll sign it."

But will she ever forgive me? Gabby asked herself.

CHAPTER TWENTY-SEVEN

IN SPITE OF its old-world reputation for vampires and werewolves, Transylvania meant simply "through the woods," and it well suited the country they were encountering. Dark green, heavily forested, steep-sided mountains and gorges were magnificent and would have been picture-perfect, even without the little waterfalls that seemed to be everywhere.

Vaughn had printed out a few pages from the Internet about the area the night before, but they stopped at the visitors center anyway to get more information and to pick up brochures.

What amazed Vaughn was that the landscape was even more striking than the professionally photographed portrayals. Film simply couldn't capture the majesty and mystery of the deep dark forests or their clean scents.

They viewed the tumbling steams of the Davidson River, the broad rock cascades of the Rainbow and Whitewater Falls and the single long drop of the Graveyard Field Falls. They oohed and aahed, clicked digital snaps of each other, even asked other tourists to take shots of them together with various falls behind them.

By four o'clock Vaughn had to admit he was beginning to fade just a little bit.

"I'm getting thirsty for those milk shakes." They'd been drinking bottled water all day. "How about you, pumpkin?"

Stephanie's eyes lit up. She wasn't about to turn down an offer like that.

On the outskirts of Brevard they found a Frosty Treat and went in, carrying the brochures with them. Stephanie ordered a chocolate ripple shake. Vaughn opted for coffee mocha.

"Been to see our falls?" the woman who was cleaning tables asked. She looked to be in her late sixties, was scrawny with crepe skin around her neck, but she had a friendly smile that was instantly winning. Her name tag identified her as Ethel.

"They're really beautiful," Stephanie said.

Ethel shifted her hip. "Which ones y'all seen?"

Vaughn recounted their itinerary.

"All right pretty," the woman agreed. "But you ain't seen my favorite. A little off the beaten track, it is, but if you have the time, it's worth the trip."

She gave Vaughn directions to Broom Falls.

"Why is it called that?" Stephanie asked. "Does it look like a broom?"

The woman smiled. "Kinda. A long thin spout, but it spreads out when it hits a rock near the bottom. I heard that *broom*'s also an old English word, or maybe it's Gaelic, that means mist. Y'all'll see why either explanation fits it when you get there."

After finishing their shakes, Vaughn thanked the woman for her help.

"Y'all come back and let me know what ya think now, hear?" she told them as they were going out the door.

Her directions were clear and easy enough to follow, except she hadn't warned him about the primitive road. They left the main highway, got onto a narrow, poorly paved lane that eventually turned to gravel and then dirt. Ethel had told him how many miles to each landmark or turnoff. Had he not found each one precisely where she said it would be, he would have turned around—if he could have found a spot wide enough—convinced he'd taken a wrong turn somewhere, though where that could have been he couldn't imagine.

"She said it was remote," he commented to his daughter. "I feel like I'm going deep into the forest primeval."

"What's primeval?"

That would teach him to use fancy words. He had to think for a few seconds. "Very old. Primitive. Like prehistoric."

"Oh." It was fairly clear that she didn't understand what prehistoric meant, either.

"Like before there were any people. In this case, a very old forest."

All at once the dense foliage overhead began to thin, sunlight dappling the coarse ribbon of dirt road, and they could make out that they were at the base of a narrow gorge.

Vaughn had been moving only about fifteen miles an hour. Now, though the way was clearer, he slowed even more. With the car windows open they could hear the rush of water, and peering through the branches of oak and maple, sycamore, hickory and hemlock, they caught their first glimpse of water cascading from a high rocky cliff on the other side of the ravine.

Ethel had said there was a place to park and turn around. She hadn't misled him so far, but Vaughn wondered if the forest might have reclaimed it since the last time she'd been here. Then, right where she'd told him it would be, he discovered a small clearing.

"Wow!" Stephanie said, looking up through the windshield.

"Yeah, wow!" Vaughn agreed. "She was right. This was worth coming to."

They got out of the Ford Explorer and approached the edge of the precipice.

"It does look like a broom," Stephanie said. "See, the water coming over the top is the handle, then it hits those rocks and fans out like bristles, and at the bottom the mist makes it look like it's sweeping dust."

He agreed. The one difference was that this dust held a rainbow.

"Let's get closer, Daddy."

She pulled him along the narrow trail that led to the base of the falls.

"Stay on this side of the stream, peanut," he said as they moved forward and he could feel the superfine spray. "We don't want to get all wet."

Before he realized it, she'd slipped her hand out of his and was moving forward.

"Steph, no. Be careful. Stay on this side."

But she was already hopping from stone to stone.

"Steph. Stop."

It was too late. One moment she was in front of him and the next…

He heard a brief cry as she slipped off a mossy rock. Then the only sound was that of the falling water.

"Stephanie…Stephanie," he yelled.

She was nowhere in sight. He shouldn't have let her run ahead like that. He should have held her hand tighter. With his left hand, not his right.

He stumbled forward over rocks that were even more

slippery than he realized. Then he saw her, crumpled between two boulders. He looked for blood but didn't see any.

"Stephanie," he shouted again. "Stephanie, are you all right?"

No answer.

"Stephanie." His shriek of her name this time was like the howl of a feral animal in pain.

He clambered down the rocks, skittered rather than climbed into the narrow crevice. Instinctively, he reached out with his right arm to gain purchase, but his fingers, lacking strength, failed to hold their grip. The weakened limb flailed and slammed into a rock. A thunderbolt of pain shot up his arm into his shoulder. He was aware of it, angered by it, but he refused to be distracted by it. His daughter was all that mattered.

Momentary relief flooded through him when he saw her chest rise and fall, but her eyes remained closed. She lay perfectly still.

He needed help, but how to get it? He removed the cell phone from his belt, flipped it open. He'd recharged it last night.

No signal.

He pressed 9-1-1 and hit the send button anyway, but there was nothing. No sound. No dial tone, not even static. He had to be crazy to think a cell phone would work in this remote area.

Using his left hand, he checked Stephanie's pulse. He couldn't find it and new panic shot through him. But she was breathing. He could see that. He checked her carotid artery again. There it was. A pulse, slow and steady.

But she was still unconscious. She must have hit her head in her fall. Did she have any broken bones? None were obvious. He ran his hands quickly along her arms and legs. No swelling. No discoloration. But it was probably too early for them to show. No groans of pain when he moved her limbs.

What other injuries could she have sustained? She needed medical attention and she needed it now.

He fought to control his panic.

CHAPTER TWENTY-EIGHT

THINK. Concentrate.

He couldn't drive all the way back to Brevard to get help. Too far. It would take too long. And suppose she woke up while he was gone and found herself all alone. If she was disoriented, she might wander off, then they'd have a new problem. What about predators? What wild animals were here? Bobcats? Mountain lions? Bears?

The forest primeval. If there were any people close by he had no idea where they might be or how to find them. He was on his own.

He reexamined his surroundings and the situation. Stephanie was in a crevice between a domed boulder and a maze of smaller rocks, many of them slick with moss. They were at least a hundred feet from the ledge where the Explorer was parked and a good fifteen feet below it. Somehow he'd have to carry his daughter to the SUV and get her to the emergency room in Brevard.

How?

And what damage might he do by moving her? Suppose her neck or spine was injured. He didn't want to think about the possibilities.

Yet what was the alternative?

With two good arms it wouldn't have been all that difficult for him to pick her up and carry her back to the car. But he didn't have two good arms. He had only one. His right arm was still screaming from the blow it had received. He could barely lift it.

Okay, he'd have to manage with only one arm. He'd do what had to be done to help his little girl. Use his bare teeth if he had to.

He repositioned her arms and legs, grabbed the back of her shirt and hauled her to the center of the boulder. Kneeling over her, he worked his good left arm under her torso, gathered her to his chest. Slowly straightening his spine, he bounced her gently so she was better poised on his shoulder. Then, struggling to maintain his equilibrium on the slippery wet rock, he carefully stood.

He would have liked to use his right arm to hold on to rocks and overhanging tree branches for balance and stability, but the pain of doing so was too distracting, too draining. He let the throbbing limb dangle at his side as he stepped catlike from one stone to another. He came to the slick-faced granite slab they'd both lost footing on. Climbing it unburdened would have been treacherous with the use of two arms. Now…

He looked frantically around and thought he saw an easier path, but it was longer and meant having to zigzag amid sharper rocks. If he slipped, if he stumbled, lost his balance and dropped her…

Heart pounding, he pressed on.

It seemed to take hours to maneuver his way back to the Explorer, even though the logical part of his brain told him only minutes had transpired. He kept listening for sounds, any sign that his daughter was rousing.

Nothing.

Not a murmur. Not a groan.

Even her breathing was silent, at least against the background of rustling trees and rushing water. Her mother had died of a head injury that he should have been able to prevent. Now his little girl.

Dear God, please let her be all right. Don't take her, too.

When he reached flat ground he was forced to use his right hand to open the rear door on the driver's side of the SUV. The pain, like a red-hot poker, brought tears to his eyes.

He laid Stephanie gently across the seat. He needed to secure her for the ride to town, so he pulled the shoulder seat belts on both sides under her and clasped them. It wasn't ideal, but it would keep her from tumbling onto the floor if he had to stop short or whip through sharp turns. He'd encountered several on the way in.

Sweating profusely in spite of the cool mountain air, he scrambled behind the wheel, started the engine with his left hand, jackknifed a U-turn and kicked up gravel leaving the waterfall.

His therapist had recommended months ago that he trade in his four-on-the-floor standard Explorer for a model with an automatic transmission. He'd balked. That would be giving in, acknowledging that he was never going to get better, that he was permanently disabled. He was a NASCAR driver, for heaven's sake. Shifting gears was part of the experience of being in control of the power under the hood.

Now he regretted his vanity. As he wove around sharp curves, ascended and descended gullies and ravines, he was constantly forced to use his right hand to shift gears to maintain optimum speed, power and control. The fingers were swelling, stiffening. He used his palm to cup the ball of the stick shift. The hand itself had no sensation now. All he felt was the searing pain in his upper arm and shoulder. It intensified with every movement as he struggled to manipulate the gearshift.

Damn the pain. He thought about the pills in his pants' pocket, but he didn't have time to stop and take one. Besides he had a feeling this time they wouldn't do any good.

He reached the gravel road, accelerated on the straightaway and looked over his shoulder at the most precious thing in his life lying on the backseat. Still no movement. Still not a sound coming from her.

Please, God, do what you will with me, but let her be safe and whole.

He slipped without conscious thought into race mode. One foot on the gas, the other on the brake pedal. He slowed at a curve, skidded through it, rebuilt speed, plunged into a narrow gulley, shot up the other side, careened through the next turn, sifted gears again, hit the tarmac and rammed his foot to the floor.

He mashed the brakes as he approached what he remembered as the next series of winding twists and turns. The heavy vehicle lurched and swayed. Did he hear a moan from the backseat?

He glanced over his shoulder. Stephanie's eyelashes fluttered. Or did they?

"Stephanie," he called, his attention again locked on the road ahead as he maneuvered another blind curve that doubled back on itself.

"Stephanie," he repeated. "Wake up, peanut."

Again they dropped into a hollow, this time so quickly, he left his stomach behind.

Another moan.

"Stephanie, wake up. Wake up, honey." Please. Please. Please.

At last he made it to the main artery into town. Traffic was heavier than it had been earlier. He refused to let it slow him. Putting on his emergency flashers, he hit the horn, flicked his high beams and roared onto the highway. The engine screamed as he slammed his way through the gears with his dead right hand. Most of the drivers in front of him jerked to the right to let him pass. He veered around the obstinate or oblivious few who didn't.

He was pretty sure he'd seen signs to a hospital on the outskirts of Brevard, but he hadn't paid much attention to them. The town was small. Finding the place couldn't be that difficult.

He caught a glimpse of a sign out of the corner of his eye as he sped along U.S. 64. Hospital Just Ahead.

He turned south at the traffic light to the sprawling single-story complex. The road took him past the main entrance to the emergency room in the rear. He began honking his horn.

"Daddy, what's happening?" She sounded sleepy, far away. "My head hurts."

A wave of relief rushed over him.

"We're at the hospital, honey. You fell and hit your head at the Broom waterfall."

"I did? I don't remember."

Hearing the horn, medical personnel in green scrubs had rushed out the back door by the time Vaughn squealed to a stop.

He opened his door and explained what had happened to the first person he encountered, a fortyish woman with a stethoscope in her hand.

"Let's get her inside," she ordered the others.

A gurney appeared and a younger man and woman helped the girl out of the backseat and onto the wheeled litter.

"Daddy?" she called, sounding frightened.

"I'm with you all the way, sweetheart. Don't worry. Everything's going to be all right." And for the first time he began to believe it actually might.

The woman with the stethoscope listened to Stephanie's heart. Her assistant put a blood pressure cuff on her wrist.

Satisfied with the readings, the physician, who identified herself as Dr. Lorette Macy, asked a series of questions while she probed and palpated.

Minutes passed. At last the physician straightened and slipped the stethoscope into her patch pocket.

"A mild concussion," she told Vaughn. "But she's alert and oriented. I'll give her some aspirin for the headache and keep her under observation for a few hours. The main thing we'll be watching for is whether she falls asleep or becomes confused. Unless either of those things happen, you can take her home, but you'll have to wake her periodically tonight to make sure she's lucid."

Finally able to breath, Vaughn thanked her profusely. Perhaps expecting him to offer his hand in gratitude, she looked at it for the first time.

"What happened to your arm?" she asked, clearly concerned.

"Just a bruise. I banged it against a rock when I was climbing." He didn't bother to mention that the pain at the moment was excruciating.

"You did more than that." With both hands she gently raised his forearm. He nearly screamed out. "Did you have a previous injury?"

He told her about the old shoulder dislocation and the resulting syndrome.

"I have some pain pills I can take," he added. "It'll be fine in a couple of hours."

"I don't think so," she said. "There's something else going on here."

CHAPTER TWENTY-NINE

"DADDY, your arm is so big." Stephanie stared at it from the examination table.

Twice its normal size, it looked as if it was about to split the seam of his shirt.

"Let's get you to the radiology suite," Macy said, "so we can do an ultrasound."

Vaughn wanted to argue. Stephanie was all right, that was all that mattered, but with that crisis past, his brain was allowing the pain in his arm to register, and it was becoming unbearable.

"You may have broken something," the doctor persisted, as she waved to an orderly to bring over the wheelchair from the corner.

Reluctantly, but with relief, Vaughn got into the chair. It was only after he was in it that he realized how weak he'd become. Adrenaline had earlier given him a burst of extraordinary energy and immunity from pain. Now that he knew Stephanie was going to be all right, everything else was catching up with him.

"Whatever it is, we'll take care of it," Dr. Macy assured the girl. "Your daddy's going to be just fine."

"I'll be okay, peanut," he added. "Don't worry."

Stephanie looked skeptical. Vaughn reached out to her

with his left hand. Before the assistant could stop her, she jumped off the table and took her father's hand in both of hers.

"That's what the doctor said when Mommy died and you got hurt." Her mouth quivered as tears dribbled down her cheeks. "But you weren't."

He hugged her shivering body as she wrapped her arms around his neck. "Everything's going to be all right, Steph. Nothing'll happen to me. I promise."

"Radiology, stat," Dr. Macy told her burly assistant whose name tag identified him as Bruce.

"I want to go, too," Stephanie insisted.

"Come on, honey." The doctor gently placed her hand on her shoulder. "You can watch while we take pictures of your daddy's arm."

Bruce pushed Vaughn's chair at a good clip, making the girl run to keep up. They went down a side corridor to a room with a sign outside warning people not to enter. The doctor opened the door, beckoned the child in, then made way for the patient in the wheelchair.

They were met by a tall, wiry man with a baby face and a shiny shaven pate. At first glance he didn't look more than thirty, but was probably closer to forty. Dr. Macy introduced the radiologist, Dr. DuKane.

"Okay, let's take a look."

Vaughn was asked to remove his shirt. Wriggling out of the left sleeve would have been easy enough, but the right one was so tight they had to cut it off. He was ordered to lie on the paper-covered examination table. His swollen and discolored right arm was positioned on a pullout extension.

The radiologist applied gel to the upper arm and shoulder and turned on the ultrasound machine. Together the four of them watched amorphous images swirl across the screen.

"I don't see any break," DuKane said. "Could be a hairline fracture, but the edema seems too extreme for that."

"Venous thrombosis?" Macy asked.

"Wh-What's that?" Stephanie asked, clearly frightened by the unfamiliar words.

"It's a blood clot, honey," the doctor explained.

As the radiologist moved the probe into Vaughn's armpit, Macy let out a soft whistle and shook her head.

"I don't think anticoagulants are going to do it with this one," she commented.

"Better call Malone," DuKane said.

She went to a telephone on the wall, dialed a single digit and asked for Dr. Malone to be paged to Radiology.

"What going on?" Vaughn asked.

"I'm calling for a consult, Mr. Steiner. Dr. Malone is our vascular surgeon. He'll be here in a minute."

"Surgeon?"

A fiftyish, heavyset man appeared almost immediately.

"I was already on my way down here to check some film when I got your page."

Macy introduced the patient.

"Vaughn Steiner. I'm Dan Malone." He stepped forward and seeing the condition of Vaughn's right hand and the little girl clinging to the left, nodded a greeting. "I've watched you race for years. Glad to meet you. Would have preferred it on your turf, though."

Vaughn thanked him and tried to smile, but the throbbing pressure in his arm was making pleasantries difficult.

Malone turned to his colleague. "What've we got?"

DuKane ran the tape he'd made of the ultrasound.

"No question," Malone said, and turned to Vaughn. "Mr. Steiner, I have good news and bad news. The bad news is you have a serious blood clot that requires immediate surgery. The good news is that you have me to perform it. I'm the best there is."

"My daughter—"

"Is there someone we can call?" Dr. Macy asked.

Vaughn thought instantly of Gabby. "Her grandmother, but she's in Greensboro."

"We'll contact her. In the meantime Stephanie will be fine here with us. We have a children's play area where she can amuse herself and we'll keep a very close eye on her."

Dr. Malone was talking on the wall phone, giving someone instruction to prepare the operating room for surgery immediately.

"Steph—" Vaughn turned to his daughter "—I don't want you to worry about me."

But the way the little girl was hanging on to him, her eyes brimming, he knew he might as well tell the rain not to fall. She was terrified, and if he was forced to tell the truth, he'd have to admit he was scared, too. He didn't want to leave her alone. All this was too much for a six-year-old. Suppose the worst happened…suppose he— He refused to complete the thought, even in his mind.

"You can do a favor for me while you're waiting, though," he said, trying to sound upbeat.

Sobbing, the girl asked, "What, Daddy? Anything?"

He detached his cell phone from his belt and handed it to her.

"I was going to call Grandma when we got here, but they don't allow people to use cell phones inside hospitals because they interfere with equipment. You'll have to go outside, turn it on—you know how—and call her. Bruce will go with you."

He looked up at the big orderly who nodded agreement.

"Tell Grandma what's happened and ask her to drive down to get you."

"But I want to stay here, with you," she pleaded.

"You can, but you shouldn't be all by yourself. I don't know how long I'll have to stay in the hospital. Ask Grandma to bring a change of clothes for me and extra clothes for the two of you. She can get a motel room here so you can visit me every day and take me home when the doctor releases me. Okay?"

She nodded. "I love you, Daddy."

"I love you, too, pumpkin. Now go with Bruce and I'll see you in a couple of hours."

GABBY WAS TURNING the corner onto the road to her condo when her cell phone chirped. She muttered a phrase of displeasure and wondered for a moment if it might be her mother. Not likely. Maybe never again. On the entire drive home from Raleigh, she kept replaying the scene in the boardroom. Vaughn's warning kept haunting her. *You'll lose something more valuable than a few million dollars.*

She was tempted to ignore the ringing and let voice mail take a message.

The entire day had been rotten. Nothing had gone right. The store she went to that morning for a promo had gotten the dates mixed up and didn't know she was coming. They did their best to accommodate her, but there had been no local publicity so the turnout had been poor—until word got out that she was there. Then, at the last minute, throngs appeared. She couldn't disappoint her fans, so she'd stayed an extra hour, putting her significantly behind schedule.

She'd left the place feeling anxious, tense, only to get out to her car to find someone had apparently backed into the rear fender on the driver's side. It wouldn't take much to repair it, but it was just another thorn in a day that seemed filled with thistles. She'd been late for her lunch appointment with Trey. Fortunately he was a patient man. Right after they ordered their food, he made his pitch. Even now thinking about it gave her a funny feeling in the pit of her stomach.

The thing about offers you couldn't refuse, she reflected, was that you couldn't refuse them. Trey had been generous, very generous. She should be grateful, and she was. So why was it leaving a funny taste in her mouth?

The phone chirped again. Heaving a sigh, she fished it out of her purse and checked the caller ID. Vaughn.

Her mood took flight. Was he calling to apologize for his knee-jerk reaction? For his serious lapse of good judgment? Did he want her to stay on the team? Had he found another sponsor for her? How should she respond?

She clicked the phone on and held it to her ear. "Hello?"

"Gabby. Gabby, it's me."

The excited sound of Stephanie's voice further lifted her spirits. Fondness for this kid over the months had grown to something more. She worried about how breaking up with Vaughn would affect her.

Then she realized that since Stephanie was calling, Vaughn wasn't. Why would Steph be calling her? Unless she'd found out about the breakup and wanted to tell her she was sad.

I am, too, kid.

"Hi, sweetie. How are you?"

"Daddy's hurt. They're operating on him."

"What?" Gabby hit the brake and pulled over to the side of the road.

"His arm. It's all my fault, Gabby. I slipped at the Broom Falls, and he hurt his arm on a rock."

The words didn't make sense. What was absolutely clear was that the child was scared.

"Steph, honey, slow down and tell we what happened. Where are you?"

"At the hospital."

"Which hospital, honey?"

"In Brevard."

"Brevard? What are you doing there?"

"We went to see the waterfalls. I fell and hit my head and Daddy had to come and get me and carry me to the car and he hurt his arm real bad. The doctor has to operate on it."

"Operate? Why, honey?"

"'Cause he's got a trombone in it. Can you come, Gabby? Please? Please?"

A trombone? It took a moment for the malapropism to clarify itself. "A thrombosis?"

"Yeah. They showed me a picture of it, but I didn't see anything. Will you come, Gabby? Oh, please?"

"Of course, I'll come, honey. Right away."

"Can you bring Grandma? Daddy wants her here but… I'm afraid if I tell her what happened to Daddy she'll get in an accident like the one we almost had on our way to Atlanta."

Gabby hadn't heard anything about a near accident on that trip. She wasn't surprised that Grace wasn't very competent behind the wheel. She struck Gabby as overly cautious and that could be as dangerous as too aggressive.

"Okay, honey. I'll call her. Who's with you now?"

"Bruce. He works here. He's real nice. He's taking care of me while they operate on Daddy."

"Okay, sweetheart. Your grandma and I will be there in a few hours. Don't worry. Everything's going to be all right."

She hoped.

Before hanging up she asked to speak to Bruce, who confirmed what she'd already figured out. He told her he had two kids of his own, one about Stephanie's age, so he'd take real good care of her.

"She's a sweet kid," he said, "and smart as a whip."

Gabby agreed, talked to Stephanie again, assured her she and her grandmother would get there as soon as they could, and reminded her if she had any questions or just wanted to talk she could call on her cell phone anytime.

Then she dialed Grace's number.

CHAPTER THIRTY

GRACE ANSWERED on the second ring. Gabby explained what had happened.

"Why did Stephanie call you? Why didn't she call me?" The questions were asked angrily, bitterly.

"She tried to but couldn't get through for some reason," Gabby lied. "You know cell phones. So she called me. The kid's pretty upset."

She was about to add that Stephanie had suggested Gabby drive her down but decided not to add insult to injury. She'd use the Atlanta trump card only if she had to. She wondered, though, if Vaughn was aware of his mother-in-law's near accident. She suspected not.

"I thought we could ride down to Brevard together."

"I'm perfectly capable of driving myself."

"There's no sense in us taking separate cars. Besides, someone will have to drive Vaughn's Explorer back. If they're doing surgery on his arm, I doubt he'll be in any shape to do it himself."

There was silence at the other end.

"This will also give us a chance to talk," Gabby added.

"About what?" When Gabby didn't immediately answer, the older woman relented, "Oh, all right. How soon will you be here?"

"I'm ten minutes away. Steph wants you to bring a change of clothes for her and her father. You should probably plan on spending a day or two down there, so pack some for yourself, as well."

Gabby hung up. She'd already decided not to bother going back to her condo. She always carried an emergency travel kit in the trunk with extra clothes and toiletries. Anything else she might need she could buy. She had her day planner, which contained all the telephone numbers she'd need to reschedule appointments or cancel them, if necesary.

Her real concerns now were Vaughn and Stephanie. His requiring surgery meant his arm had deteriorated. Would he lose more use of it, be left even more handicapped than he already was?

What would his reaction be when he saw her at the hospital? Glad to see her? Angry at her being there? Would he greet her as a friend and a lover or as someone who had deceived him?

And how would he accept her news about Trey?

So many questions. So much uncertainty.

The moment Gabby pulled into the driveway Grace opened the front door, set an overnight-sized piece of luggage at her feet and locked the door. Gabby relieved her of the bag and put it in the trunk while Grace got into the passenger seat.

Initially they discussed what Gabby knew about the accident, which wasn't much more than she'd already passed on. Grace had tried to call Stephanie on Vaughn's cell phone but got voice mail instead of a pick up.

"Probably has to keep it turned off inside the hospital," Gabby explained.

"This is my fault," Grace muttered. "I kept pushing Vaughn to spend more time with Stephanie."

"That was the right thing to do," Gabby said. "As far as this accident is concerned, I doubt it was anybody's fault. Something like it could have happened anywhere, anytime. You certainly have nothing to blame yourself for. You were thinking of your granddaughter, so was Vaughn. She really is a very special kid."

"Lisa is losing her. Losing her and Vaughn."

Gabby considered the words. It was a strange way to phrase it, but Gabby thought she understood what the older woman meant. Suddenly Grace's coldness over the past months began to make sense. She saw Gabby as an interloper, someone who was going to supplant her daughter.

"I want Stephanie to remember her mother," Grace added, "not replace her with someone else."

Like me.

"No one's trying to replace your daughter, Grace. I'm certainly not. Lisa was Stephanie's mother. Nothing will ever change that and Steph is old enough to have a clear memory of her. She won't forget. Lisa taught her what it's like to be loved, to be happy. No matter who comes into her life Lisa will always be Stephanie's mommy."

Grace remained silent. Even without looking over, Gabby could feel her sadness and uncertainty.

"As for Vaughn, you don't have to worry about him forgetting Lisa, either. She was the mother of his child. There's no question he loved her very much. Nothing will ever change that."

They drove on in the midst of an unending stampede of long-haul truckers.

"Lisa will live forever in their memories, Grace, just as

she does in yours. Any woman who'd try to replace her would be a fool. After all, take away Lisa and you change who Vaughn and Stephanie are."

She let the thought linger before she went on. "But they also need more than memories. They need to get on with their lives, not dwell on the past."

Gabby felt the other woman turn and stare at her. She wasn't certain if it was with hostility or if she was merely shocked by what Gabby had said.

They retreated into silence for several miles. Grace probably assumed Gabby was pleading for herself. In fact she wasn't. Vaughn had made it clear he had no interest in her as a permanent part of his life or Stephanie's. As painful as his rejection was, she didn't hate him. What she'd just told his mother-in-law was true, and she hoped one day he'd find a woman whom he did want to be a full partner in his life and family. She'd thought for a while she could fill that role, but somehow she'd failed.

"What about you and Trey?" Grace asked as they began their ascent toward the Great Smokey Mountains and the city of Ashville.

"Trey?" What could Grace possibly know about him? "What about him?"

"I saw the picture in *The Chatterer* of you two laughing and holding hands."

Gabby cocked an eyebrow. Grace didn't strike her as someone who followed gossip columns or read sensational tabloids.

"Pictures can be deceiving."

"You were having dinner with him, weren't you?" Grace asked, her tone accusatory.

"He's a friend of the family. What has my having dinner with him got to do with anything?"

"Your mother told me you're getting engaged."

Gabby nearly slammed on the brakes. "She said what?"

Grace seemed confused by Gabby's reaction. "Your mother said you and Trey have been seeing each other for months and that you'll soon be announcing your engagement to be married. Della's thrilled about it, by the way. She's very happy for you."

Gabby's mind was in a whirlwind. She tightened her grip on the steering wheel and tried to sort out what was going on.

"When did she tell you this?"

"Why...the morning the picture was published. She said she suspected the two of you have been seeing each other."

That was when Gabby began to put things in chronological order and it all became clear. She began to laugh.

Grace looked over as if she were losing her mind.

Maybe she was.

CHAPTER THIRTY-ONE

THE TOWN OF BREVARD was in as beautiful a setting as any Gabby had ever seen. Densely green-covered mountains peaked and towered around it. Finding the hospital wasn't difficult. She pulled into the parking lot in front and the two of them walked quickly to the main entrance. The air was cool and heavy with humidity, but it was also scented with the spicy nighttime tang of mountain pine.

A woman with bluish silver hair sitting at a reception desk greeted them with a smile that could have conveyed pleasure or sympathy. "May I help you?"

"We're looking for Vaughn Steiner. He was brought in—"

"Oh, yes. Mr. Steiner. My grandson's a big fan." Her eyes brightened even more. "You're Gabby O'Farrell, aren't you? Mr. Steiner's daughter told us you were coming. I have to tell you she thinks the world of you."

"That's very kind of you."

"About Mr. Steiner…" Grace reminded her.

"Yes, yes, of course." She told them the room number.

"And Stephanie?" Gabby asked.

"She's with him, I imagine. Such a nice little girl. So polite."

They followed the receptionist's directions and found themselves at a nurses' station, which at the moment appeared to be unattended. Signs on the wall clearly indicated the location of rooms by number. The two women turned right. Vaughn's name was on a door halfway down the wide corridor. It was slightly ajar. Gabby pushed it open the rest of the way.

Stephanie was straddling a steel straight-backed chair facing the bed, while an older woman sat in a similar chair behind her, brushing her hair. When light from the bright hallway entered the dimmer room, the girl jumped up, ran to Gabby and threw her arms around her waist. "I knew you'd come. I knew you would."

Hands crossed on the girl's back, Gabby glanced over and caught the hurt expression on Grace's face. Her granddaughter hadn't run to her, as she'd no doubt expected and felt she deserved.

"We got here as soon as we could," Gabby said, subtly slipped out of the girl's grasp and nudged her toward Grace. Stephanie wrapped her arms around her grandmother and said, "Oh, Grandma. I was so scared."

The woman in the second chair had by this time slowly risen. "You're in good hands now, darling," she said, "So I'll be on my way."

"Who are you?" Grace asked in not the friendliest of tones.

"Ethel is the lady who told us about Broom Falls," Stephanie explained. "It was awesome."

Ethel stroked her bony hand over Stephanie's hair. "I never would've sent them there if I'd known this was going to happen. I feel so bad. Soon as I heard, I had to come. Figured she could use some company." She reached for the tote she'd placed on the bed's tray table and put the brush she'd been using in it. "I'll be going now. Sure hope everything turns out all right."

"Thank you for doing my hair," Stephanie said.

The woman smiled. "Pshaw. A girl's got to keep up her appearances. Nothing like a nice warm shampoo to make you feel better." She clutched the bag at her waist with both hands. "I hope I'll get to see y'all again sometime," she said to Stephanie.

Gabby moved toward the door with Ethel and thanked her for coming.

"You got a really good kid there. Take good care of her now." The woman stepped outside and was gone.

"Are you all right, sweetheart?" Grace asked her granddaughter. "Tell me exactly what happened."

"We went to see Broom Falls and I slipped on a rock and banged my head. The doctor said I might have a con-con—"

"A concussion? Oh, darling..." Grace stroked Stephanie's hair the way Ethel had a few minutes earlier—it shone like spun gold.

"But she says I'm all right now. I don't have a headache anymore, and I didn't fall asleep like they were afraid I would, even though I got tired just sitting around waiting for Daddy to come out of the operating room."

"How is he?" Grace asked.

"He's fine," a voice said from the bed.

They all turned, till then unaware the patient was awake. In spite of the scratchiness in his voice, the notes of pleasure and humor were unmistakable.

His gaze met Gabby's. "Thanks for coming."

"I just happened to be in the neighborhood."

"Uh-huh." He closed his eyes but his lips formed a faint smile.

"Vaughn, what in the world happened?" Grace demanded. "I mean, your arm."

His right shoulder and upper arm were heavily bandaged but not in a cast.

As if it took tremendous effort, he reopened his eyes. "Venous thrombosis in the armpit. They had to go in surgically to remove the blood clot. The doc tells me he got it all and that I'm going to be fine."

"You're certain?"

Vaughn made a gruff chuckling sound. "No, but Dr. Malone is. He assures me he's the greatest surgeon in the world, especially when it comes to venous thrombosis. Thromboses? Whatever. He's God's gift to the world of surgery, so I'm going to be as good as new. Maybe better."

Grace gave him a mixed smile of doubt and encouragement.

They visited a few minutes more, he and Stephanie taking turns describing the things they'd seen and, of course, her fall. Gabby noted that he said simply that he'd carried her to the car and rushed back to town, but she knew it couldn't have been that easy.

"His arm was so big when we got here," Stephanie explained, "that they had to cut his shirt off with scissors. It must have really, really hurt, but Daddy didn't even complain."

"I think he was more worried about you, honey," Gabby said, looking over at him, her heart aching with love, admiration and her own sense of failure to keep him. "That's the way dads are."

Conversation dwindled, and the room was suddenly

filled with silence. Everyone seemed to shift self-consciously in unison.

"Grace," Vaughn finally said, "would you mind taking Steph to the cafeteria? Everybody here has been great, but she needs to eat something more substantial than soda and chips."

His mother-in-law nodded and placed her hands on Stephanie's shoulders. "That's what grandmothers are for, putting meat on skinny bones. Come on, girl, let's go see if we can find you some tofu and sauerkraut to balance your diet."

"Grandma!" Stephanie looked up at her in horror.

"Well, maybe pizza, then."

Stephanie's eyes lit up in wonder. "Really? With pepperoni?" she asked, clearly worried she might be pushing the envelope.

Grace rolled her eyes heavenward and clicked her tongue. "With pepperoni."

Gabby and Vaughn both had raised eyebrows as the two left the room.

"What in the world did you say to the woman on the trip down here?" Vaughn asked. "I think that's the first joke I've ever heard her crack."

Gabby was surprised herself. Their discussion had been so intense and the look of hurt in the woman's eyes when her granddaughter ran to Gabby instead of to her seemed to contradict her sudden discovery of mirth.

Just when you think you have people pegged, they surprise you.

"Search me."

"Pull up a chair and sit down a spell," he said.

She did, but couldn't relax.

"I owe you an apology," Vaughn said.

Realizing the surprises weren't over, Gabby leaned back and crossed her arms. "About what?"

"You deserve better of me than what I gave you. You were right. I should have shown more faith in you. You've done an incredible job on the track, as good as any rookie and considerably better than most. You're dedicated. You have determination. You've put everything you've got into winning."

"You're beginning to sound like a politician."

"That's not the pattern of a dilettante," he went on, ignoring her comment.

"Dilettante?"

"You're mother said you wouldn't stay with racing—"

"My mother doesn't know me, doesn't understand me. She never has. She loves me. She has my best interests at heart. I don't doubt that, but she really doesn't understand me."

"I can see that now." He pressed the button on the bed rail and raised the back a little more. The sleepiness was gone from his eyes and his voice. He was wide awake now. More than awake, alive, restless.

"I owe you an apology for misjudging you," he repeated. "I hope you'll forgive me."

She cast him an affectionate smile. "Apology accepted."

"As for racing—" he shifted his good left shoulder "—I'd like you to stay with the team next year, if you want to. I'll find you another sponsor."

"We need to talk some more about that. But there's something I'd like to get straight first."

She met his gaze, locked on to it.

"I need to know about our personal relationship, Vaughn. What about us?"

CHAPTER THIRTY-TWO

"WHY DIDN'T YOU want to have anything more to do with me after my mother reneged on OI's sponsorship?" she asked.

"It wasn't because she reneged. I was working on getting you another sponsor, and I would have, but then Della showed up and told me you were going to marry this David guy, and that he would put the kibosh on you driving stock cars. So what was the point?"

"My mother has a big mouth."

She stood and moved over to the window. Sodium vapor lights cast the long, green lawn in an eerie yellow glow. A car was pulling up the driveway toward the entrance. But she wasn't interested in what was out there.

"She's also fantasizing, Vaughn. I told you my mother doesn't understand me. The only one who ever did was my dad. And I thought you." She leaned against the ledge, facing him. "Why didn't you just ask me if any of it was true? After the way my mother stabbed me—and you—in the back, why were you willing to take her word about something this important without even giving me a chance to explain? Did you really think I was sleeping with you at the same time I was about to get engaged to someone else? Or did you think I was sleeping with him, too?"

His only response was to turn his head away.

"Do you really think that little of me, Vaughn?"

"Why didn't you tell me you were seeing Trey David?" he returned. "It would have been nice if you'd kept me informed about what was going on, too, especially since it was apparently so innocent."

"Apparently?" she repeated.

"You had plenty of opportunities to explain, Gabby, if you'd wanted to. What was I supposed to think?"

"Well, excuse me. Am I not allowed to have dinner with a friend without being romantically involved with him? Or without asking your permission? You're right. We ought to cool this whole relationship if you're going to turn into a control freak."

"What about the picture in *The Chatterer?* You sure looked like you were having a pretty good time, holding his hand."

Jealousy. The green-eyed monster. Somehow it reassured her. It was dangerous, but it also made her feel special.

"We weren't holding hands. The camera just caught us at an angle that made it look that way."

"Still, you never mentioned him to me. Why? Even when your picture is splashed all over a scandal sheet, you didn't think I had a right to a tip-off? An explanation? Even if you didn't care about me, do you have any idea what kind of damage that picture could have done to you professionally? It sure wouldn't make getting you a new sponsor easier."

"Is that all you were worried about, my career? Your precious team?"

His eyes narrowed; his lips tightened. His voice, already low, had turned even softer.

"So this really is about you? Not about your career. Not

about the team. Not about us. About you. I guess your mother was right on that score, at least."

It felt like a slap. A slap that hurt.

"I'm a professional, Vaughn, and don't you ever doubt that." She had to admit, though, that from his perspective it probably looked as though she was playing games. Why hadn't she told him about Trey? She'd told Trey about him. "I care very much about my career, my long-term career, and about the team, but we were talking about us. About you and me. Remember?"

"I still don't understand your relationship with Trey David," he said.

"Look, Trey happens to be a genuinely nice guy, and I have to admit, if I weren't in love with you and he didn't already have a girlfriend, I might be tempted."

Vaughn sat there, wide-eyed, staring. "You're in love with me?"

She came up to the left side of the bed and placed her hand on his shoulder, then leaned down and kissed him softly on the lips. "Of course I'm in love with you, you idiot. Why do you think I've been sleeping with you?"

"But then why—" He was touching her face, studying her features with eyes and hand.

"Was I out with him? Strictly business. He happens to be Emporico's vice president in charge of public relations. He's also in control of millions—tens of millions of promotional dollars."

"Including sponsorships," Vaughn mumbled after a long silence, but the volume had risen.

"Oh, I see the anesthetic is finally beginning to wear off." She grinned as she shook her head. "When I found out Mom was dumping me and that, thanks to her putting out the word, other companies weren't jumping at the chance to sponsor me, I decided to explore other options. I had dinner with Trey and he told me Emporico might be interested."

"You could have told me."

"I should have. I wish now I had, but I really wasn't sure if anything would come of it. I didn't want to disappoint you if it didn't work out, and…well…I didn't want to look like a failure. If I succeeded, I figured it would be a wonderful surprise." She heaved a breath. "Unfortunately, it seems to have backfired."

He frowned. "I should have had more faith, trusted you more."

"Yeah, you should have." She leaned over and kissed him again, this time lingering longer. "But I should have been more forthcoming, too. I'm sorry."

"I am, too. I love you, Gabby. It hurt to think you might be… So is he? Interested in sponsoring you, I mean?"

She laughed. "For the next three years, at least. We're discussing options for the years after that now."

"You're incredible." He ran a finger along her chin. "I approached Emporico fifteen months ago when I was hunting for sponsors. Got turned down flat."

"That was when Oneida Gilbert was still in charge, before Trey took over."

"What about your mom? Does she know about this?"

Gabby shook her head. "At the moment I don't think she's particularly interested, much less thrilled for me."

Gabby told him about the meeting she and Desmond Fairchild had had with Della that afternoon.

"Pretty serious stuff," he said sympathetically. "Are the two of you going to be able to heal the rift?"

"We will eventually. Or at least we'll pretend we have."

"I'm sorry," he said.

She smiled ruefully. "It was inevitable, I think. We've never seen eye to eye. I've disappointed her. I'm not a fine lady. Worse, I have no desire to be. Sure, I've been a... What did you call me? A dilettante. That was because I was searching for something I couldn't name, couldn't put my finger on. But I know what it is now. I want to be a race car driver. I want to drive around in circles at a hundred-and-eighty miles an hour and end up in Victory Lane. And I want to love you. I want you to love me."

He kissed her hand. "I can't guarantee you Victory Lane, Gabby, but I can guarantee you that I love you. And I always will."

EPILOGUE

"COME ON. Come on, come on," Vaughn shouted, shaking his fists in front of him. "Come on, sweetheart, come on. Yes!" He threw both hands up over his head in a salute of triumph.

The roar of the crowd threatened to drown out the scream of forty-three unmuffled high-performance engines running full-open. Everyone on both sides of the track cheered as Gabby received the checkered flag.

"She won!" Stephanie was jumping up and down. "Daddy, Gabby won! She won, Grandma. Gabby won."

People were slapping Vaughn and Mack on the back. The two men were slapping each other on the back. The stands were going wild.

For the first time in history a woman had won the NASCAR NEXTEL Cup!

The PA system blared the news, but no one was listening. They already knew. The question on everybody's lips all day had been whether she could pull it off. One hundred-and-seventy-five thousand fans had witnessed it in person. Another fifty million or so had seen it on TV. Gabby O'Farrell had just won the highest prize in stock car racing. Jem Nordstrom came in second.

While she made her victory lap, everyone in the infield

started migrating toward Victory Lane. The long rituals of championship were about to commence.

The noise from the bleachers continued even as the roar and rumble of mighty engines diminished and the only one that could be heard in the clamor was that of Number 111.

GABBY'S TEAM and friends gathered around her. Vaughn, Stephanie, Grace, Mack and the entire crew. Even Trey David and his fiancée, Bliss, were there, clapping and cheering as she climbed out of the stock car window.

Della was there, as well. Just as Gabby had predicted, she'd signed the letter of resignation as CEO of OI, and ten days ago, after six weeks of defiance, had made a truce with her daughter, thanks to the intercession of Trey David and Desmond Fairchild. The two women were polite but cool to each other in private, while in public the president of OI played her roles as executive and mother in award-winning fashion.

Champagne spouted.

When it was time for the award of the NASCAR NEXTEL Cup, Gabby kissed her mother in a way that left no doubt of its sincerity.

The trophy was presented, speeches were made, acknowledgments voiced. Then came the photo ops. With her team. With her owner. With her sponsor, who also happened to be her mother. With her owner's daughter. Even with his mother-in-law. With various other sponsors' representatives, this time including Trey David who took the opportunity to announce that Emporico would be her sponsor next year.

For Gabby it should have been exhausting, but there was too much adrenaline flowing to feel fatigue, to feel anything but an almost numbing sense of joy.

Gabby O'Farrell had won the NASCAR NEXTEL Cup in her rookie season. It didn't get any better than that.

Hours passed before she was at last set free by friends and admirers, by fans and media who couldn't seem to get enough of her. She was still smiling broadly when Vaughn finally came to drag her away. She signed one more autograph, thanked the fan who had waited for hours to ambush her, and in the next second Vaughn had her by the hand and was running with her toward the motor coaches.

His was the closest and he pulled her into it.

"What are we doing here?" she asked. "Everybody is over in my place."

He shut the door behind her and took her hands in his. He'd regained considerable strength in his right hand since the operation in Brevard. Apparently the surgeon had been as good as he claimed. He'd found the damaged nerve that was the source of Vaughn's problem and repaired it. The chronic pain had miraculously disappeared and with physical therapy his might and dexterity were increasing.

"I have something important to ask you," he said to Gabby.

She looked baffled, and for some unaccountable reason her heart began to thrum. "Oh?"

He gently massaged her hands in is. "Gabby, will you marry me?"

It could have been pure exhaustion that had her knees turning to liquid, that had her whole body experiencing a sudden onset of weakness. But it wasn't exhaustion and it wasn't weakness that possessed her at that moment, because that wouldn't explain the lightheaded exhilaration that went with it.

She opened her mouth, but no sounds came out.

"I promise to love, honor and cherish you for as long as I live, Gabby. I love you."

Since she still wasn't able to enunciate words, she did the only thing left to do. She threw her arms around his neck, pulled herself up against him and kissed him hard on the lips.

When they finally broke off, breathless, he held her by the waist and leaned back. Eyes twinkling, he said, "Does that mean yes?"

She nodded as tears welled.

They kissed again.

"We have the potential for mothers-in-law from hell, you know that, I suppose."

She laughed. "Don't worry about Mom. When she sees how well OI is doing after my victory today, she'll mellow. NASCAR fans are extremely loyal, and big dividends always win her approval."

He chuckled. "She's already let it be known—to Mack, not to me—that OI might be interested in being a secondary sponsor on both your car and Brett's."

"You're kidding." Gabby grinned from ear to ear. "As for Grace, we've already seen her soften her attitude."

"You still haven't said it," Vaughn told her.

She wrinkled her brow. "It? Oh, you mean that I love you?" She narrowed her eyes, those beautiful blue eyes. Her lips twitched playfully. "I love you with all my heart, Vaughn Steiner."

They walked hand-in-hand to her coach and were greeted by friends and family.

"Well, Gabriella," Della said quietly after another round of congratulations for her big win and a toast with champagne, "you've accomplished what you set out to do. Now what are you going to do with the rest of your life?"

Gabby wrapped her arm around Vaughn's, peered into his soft brown eyes. "Oh, I'll think of something."

A minute later Vaughn, showing an unexpected flair for the dramatic, struck everyone dumb when he got down on one knee in front of Gabby and asked her to marry him, this time holding out a huge diamond solitaire. She laughed, even as tears spilled down her cheeks. He crooked an eyebrow and she said yes.

Which brought a new round of cheers and congratulations.

Della kissed her daughter, said the appropriate words, then moved off to the side to make room for other well-wishers. She was nursing a flute of champagne when, a few minutes later, Gabby came up to her.

"Mom, I was wondering if you would do something for me."

"What's that, darling?"

"Take charge of the wedding arrangements for me. You know what a klutz I am about social formalities."

Della's face lit up. "Of course, I will, sweetheart. After all, I have the time now." At Gabby's hurt expression she smiled, deposited her glass on the nearby counter and put her arms around her daughter and gave her an enthusiastic hug. "We'll do it up right."

That was when Gabby knew she was in for it, but this time it made her grin.

Her mother gazed at her intently for a minute. "I hope you'll be happy, Gabriella. I truly do. I just wish your father could be here to walk you down the aisle."

"He will be, Mom. He'll be right by my side."

Della called Stephanie over and asked her if she would

like to be the flower girl. Stephanie was clapping her hands when her father joined them. Gabby explained what they had been discussing.

Bouncing on her feet, Stephanie looked up at Gabby. "When you get back from your honeymoon—" something Gabby hadn't even thought about yet "—will you teach me how to drive a race car? Please?"

* * * * *

Mediterranean Nights

Join the guests and crew of Alexandra's Dream, *the newest luxury ship to set sail on the romantic Mediterranean, as they experience the glamorous world of cruising.*

A new Harlequin continuity series
begins in June 2007 with
FROM RUSSIA, WITH LOVE
by Ingrid Weaver

Marina Artamova books a cabin on the luxurious cruise ship Alexandra's Dream, *when she finds out that her orphaned nephew and his adoptive father are aboard. She's determined to be reunited with the boy...but the romantic ambience of the ship and her undeniable attraction to a man she considers her enemy are about to interfere with her quest!*

Turn the page for a sneak preview!

Piraeus, Greece

"THERE SHE IS, Stefan. *Alexandra's Dream.*" David Anderson squatted beside his new son and pointed at the dark blue hull that towered above the pier. The cruise ship was a majestic sight, twelve decks high and as long as a city block. A circle of silver and gold stars, the logo of the Liberty Cruise Line, gleamed from the swept-back smokestack. Like some legendary sea creature born for the water, the ship emanated power from every sleek curve—even at rest it held the promise of motion. "That's going to be our home for the next ten days."

The child beside him remained silent, his cheeks working in and out as he sucked furiously on his thumb. Hair so blond it appeared white ruffled against his forehead in the harbor breeze. The baby-sweet scent unique to the very young mingled with the tang of the sea.

"Ship," David said. "Uh, *parakhod.*"

From beneath his bangs, Stefan looked at the *Alexandra's Dream.* Although he didn't release his thumb, the corners of his mouth tightened with the beginning of a smile.

David grinned. That was Stefan's first smile this afternoon, one of only two since they had left the orphanage yesterday. It was probably because of the boat—according to the orphanage staff, the boy loved boats, which was the main reason David had decided to book this cruise. Then again, there was a strong possibility the smile could have been a reaction to David's attempt at pocket-dictionary Russian. Whatever the cause, it was a good start.

The liaison from the adoption agency had claimed that Stefan had been taught some English, but David had yet to see evidence of it. David continued to speak, positive his son would understand his tone even if he couldn't grasp the words. "This is her maiden voyage. Her first trip, just like this is our first trip, and that makes it special." He motioned toward the stage that had been set up on the pier beneath the ship's bow. "That's why everyone's celebrating."

The ship's official christening ceremony had been held the day before and had been a closed affair, with only the cruise-line executives and VIP guests invited, but the stage hadn't yet been disassembled. Banners bearing the blue and white of the Greek flag of the ship's owner, as well as the Liberty circle of stars logo, draped the edges of the platform. In the center, a group of musicians and a dance troupe dressed in traditional white folk costumes performed for the benefit of the *Alexandra's Dream*'s first passengers. Their audience was in a festive mood, snapping their fingers in time to the music while the dancers twirled and wove through their steps.

David bobbed his head to the rhythm of the mandolins. They were playing a folk tune that seemed vaguely familiar, possibly from a movie he'd seen. He hummed a few notes. "Catchy melody, isn't it?"

Stefan turned his gaze on David. His eyes were a striking shade of blue, as cool and pale as a winter horizon and far too solemn for a child not yet five. Still, the smile that hovered at the corners of his mouth persisted. He moved his head with the music, mirroring David's motion.

David gave a silent cheer at the interaction. Hopefully, this cruise would provide countless opportunities for more. "Hey, good for you," he said. "Do you like the music?"

The child's eyes sparked. He withdrew his thumb with a pop. *"Moozika!"*

"Music. Right!" David held out his hand. "Come on, let's go closer so we can watch the dancers."

Stefan grasped David's hand quickly, as if he feared it would be withdrawn. In an instant his budding smile was replaced by a look close to panic.

Did he remember the car accident that had killed his parents? It would be a mercy if he didn't. As far as David knew, Stefan had never spoken of it to anyone. Whatever he had seen had made him run so far from the crash that the police hadn't found him until the next day. The event had traumatized him to the extent that he hadn't uttered a word until his fifth week at the orphanage. Even now he seldom talked.

David sat back on his heels and brushed the hair from Stefan's forehead. That solemn, too-old gaze locked with his and, for an instant, David felt as if he looked back in time at an image of himself thirty years ago.

He didn't need to speak the same language to understand exactly how this boy felt. He knew what it meant to be alone and powerless among strangers, trying to be brave and tough but wishing with every fiber of his being for a place to belong, to be safe, and most of all for someone to love him....

He knew in his heart he would be a good parent to Stefan. It was why he had never considered halting the adoption process after Ellie had left him. He hadn't balked when he'd learned of the recent claim by Stefan's spinster aunt, either; the absentee relative had shown up too late for her case to be considered. The adoption was meant to be. He and this child already shared a bond that went deeper than paperwork or legalities.

A seagull screeched overhead, making Stefan start and press closer to David.

"That's my boy," David murmured. He swallowed hard, struck by the simple truth of what he had just said.

That's my *boy.*

"I CAN'T BE PATIENT, RUDOLPH. I'm not going to stand by and watch my nephew get ripped from his country and his roots to live on the other side of the world."

Rudolph hissed out a slow breath. "Marina, I don't like the sound of that. What are you planning?"

"I'm going to talk some sense into this American kidnapper."

"No. Absolutely not. No offence, but diplomacy is not your strong suit."

"Diplomacy be damned. Their ship's due to sail at five o'clock."

"Then you wouldn't have an opportunity to speak with him even if his lawyer agreed to a meeting."

"I'll have ten days of opportunities, Rudolph, since I plan to be on board that ship."

* * * * *

Follow Marina and David as they join forces to uncover the reason behind little Stefan's unusual silence, and the secret behind the death of his parents....

Look for FROM RUSSIA, WITH LOVE by Ingrid Weaver in stores June 2007.